CENTRAL LIBRARY
ROMANCE
20 FEB 2015
27 OCT 2015
AUG 2016
20 SEP 2
D0835547
WITHDRAWN

Inverclyde Libraries
34106 003129645

It could only be for tonight. For old times' sake, she reasoned silently. There was no chance of anything more.

They had tried that and it didn't work. She wasn't going there again. She wasn't giving up her dreams for this man. But she knew her heart was finally out of harm's way—it was safely tucked inside the walls that she had erected when she'd walked out and left him—so she gave in to her desires. It would just be one night, she reassured herself.

He was staring straight at her with his bedroom eyes. Despite wondering if she was about to make one of life's bad decisions and one she might just regret, she seemed powerless to stop. Was it lust or was it love? She wasn't sure, but it was going to happen.

'Don't tell me to stop. I know what I'm about to do—' she started.

Suddenly her words were cut short by his lips pressing against hers. His hands gently cupped her face as his mouth captured her sigh. She didn't fight him. She didn't want to talk any more. Her hands instinctively reached up and pulled him closer. Her body arched with desire. She was aflame with the heat in his fingers as his hands slid under her clothing to stroke her bare skin. His kisses became more urgent and she opened her mouth to him. She wanted to feel him, to have him, just once more.

Dear Reader

I am so happy to bring you this story of love the second time around.

Tom and Sara are two very dedicated doctors who fell in love but have been driven apart by a secret in Tom's past that has prevented him from fulfilling Sara's dream for their future. Sara has walked away from their marriage still deeply in love but not willing to sacrifice her needs. For the first time in her life she's made a stand—even though it has broken her heart.

Fate brings them together three years later and they quickly discover the passion they shared is still very much present. But so are their differences.

Circumstance finds them spending four weeks working together, and they must make a choice: to fight their desire and continue on different paths leading away from each other or to surrender to their longings and find a way forward in each other's arms.

Tom and Sara are two wonderfully strong characters, and I hope you enjoy reading about their journey to find happiness as much as I loved writing this second chapter to their special love story.

Love really can be rekindled...it just takes faith, honesty and two pure hearts.

Susanne Hampton

BACK IN HER HUSBAND'S ARMS

BY

SUSANNE HAMPTON

Published in Great Britain 2014
by Mills & Boon, an imprint of Harlequin (UK) Limited,
Eton House, 18-24 Paradise Road, Richmond, Surrey, TW9 1SR

ISBN: 978 0 263 24248 5

Harlequin (UK) Limited's policy is to use papers that are natural, renewable and recyclable products and made from wood grown in sustainable forests. The logging and manufacturing processes conform to the legal environmental regulations of the country of origin.

Printed and bound in Great Britain
by CPI Antony Rowe, Chippenham, Wiltshire

Married to the man she met at eighteen, **Susanne Hampton** is the mother of two adult daughters—one a musician and the other an artist.

The family also extends to a slightly irritable Maltese shih-tzu, a neurotic poodle, three elderly ducks and four hens that only very occasionally bother to lay eggs. Susanne loves everything romantic and pretty, so her home is brimming with romance novels, movies and shoes.

With an interest in all things medical, her career has been in the dental field and the medical world in different roles, and now Susanne has taken that love into writing Mills & Boon® Medical Romance™.

A recent title by Susanne Hampton:

UNLOCKING THE DOCTOR'S HEART

These books are also available in eBook format from www.millsandboon.co.uk

Dedication

To the very special women in my life
who have helped me through life's challenging times
and made me stronger.

Your friendship is more precious than diamonds
and a treasure greater than gold.

And to Charlotte for being the most amazing editor…
thank you for your unlimited patience
and encouragement.

CHAPTER ONE

SARA FIELDING MADE her way along the wet footpath, dodging the small potholes that had filled with water from the overnight rain, her feet tucked inside flat knee-high boots. It was eight in the morning and bitterly cold. She tugged her collar up against the breeze that was cutting through her heavy overcoat, wishing she had worn her woollen tights.

Winter mornings in Melbourne were brutal, she remembered, and today was no exception. It had been thundering down when her plane had landed only an hour before and she had caught a cab straight into the city. The rain had paused momentarily but the overcast sky promised another downpour at any moment. Her favourite pair of brown leather gloves were only just preventing her fingers from freezing around the handle of her briefcase, so she quickly picked up her pace. She didn't want to arrive at the hospital soaked to the bone.

Sara had been living in Adelaide for the last three years and this was only her second trip back to Melbourne in all that time. The first had been four weeks ago when she'd travelled over to finalise her visa at the American embassy. Sara had had serious reservations about returning to Melbourne at all. She would have preferred any other city, but it was the United States embassy that processed South Australian visa applications. She'd had no choice.

Melbourne held wonderful memories but also a sadness that she really didn't want to face. She had told herself it was only an overnight stay. A quick trip. Nothing to worry about. But now, looking back, she realised she should have listened to her intuition and stayed far away from the town where Tom Fielding still lived. She was already planning a new life in Texas. So much further from Melbourne. So much further from the temptation of Tom Fielding.

She now knew that she couldn't trust her heart, or her body for that matter, around the man. He wasn't a bad man, quite the opposite, in fact, but he was definitely the wrong man for her. Against her will, Sara's thoughts were dragged back to that brief trip and how terribly wrong it had all gone.

Day one had been fine. The visa application had been processed without any hiccups. It had been day two when Sara had found herself sitting alone at Vue de Monde on the fifty-fifth floor of the historic Rialto building. She had ordered her meal and had been in high spirits, sipping her white wine and thinking about her impending trip to Texas.

She had been offered a position at a large teaching hospital in San Antonio. It was going to be a fresh start, a chance to move on and find a life that might just fulfil her dreams. Sara had finally grown tired of her life revolving around what everyone else wanted. Sacrificing her dreams, her hopes, for the needs of everyone else had become a pattern until three years ago. That fateful day when she'd decided she couldn't give up on one particular dream. She hoped this move would give her the chance to realise that dream. The dream of becoming a mother. She knew she had the packing, the shipping and all that a move of that distance entailed, but it would be worth every bit of effort. She would be free to live her life on her terms.

Suddenly her thoughts were stolen. As was her breath. Both taken by the vision of a man she'd thought she would never see again.

Sara did a double take. *Could it be?* She shook her head a little. *Could it really be him?*

He walked into the restaurant and took a seat at a table by the window. It had been three years since she had last seen him. They hadn't contacted each other since she'd left. No telephone calls. No letters. Nothing.

Perhaps it was her imagination. Perhaps it was someone who looked just like him.

Then she reminded herself there was really no other man who came close to his looks, his stature, his charisma. It was definitely Tom Fielding. All six foot two inches of him had crossed the room and had turned every woman's head as he'd done so.

Sara's heart raced a little as she watched him take the wine list from the waitress. She saw the waitress attempt to flirt, it was subtle, but enough for another woman to notice. Tom was unmoved. He didn't appear to notice or, if he did, he didn't respond. The flustered waitress placed the napkin in his lap and hovered, a little longer than necessary.

Sara felt a tightening in her chest and butterflies awakening in the pit of her stomach as the reality of being this close to Tom hit home. She had forgotten the effect he had on her. And apparently still did. Her emotions began playing havoc, sending her mind into a tailspin. She looked away. Swallowing hard, she began to play with her cutlery absent-mindedly.

She hadn't expected so many mixed emotions to come in to play. Attraction, regret, melancholy, guilt, even a hint of lust. This was not supposed to happen. This was a bad dream playing out. Sharing the same restaurant as Tom was not in the plan, and her options to escape the uncomfortable situation were limited. She could hardly leave the restaurant after ordering her dinner. Most likely it would draw even more attention to her. She didn't want to look back in Tom's direction but she was drawn to him. Drawn to him just like the conflicting desire to gaze at an open wound.

Tom chose a wine and handed the waitress back the wine list. He looked out the window across the sweeping views of the Melbourne skyline. The panorama of lights all twinkling against the black sky. Then he turned in his seat, just a little, but enough to see Sara.

He didn't move. He froze in his chair, staring in silence. Sara did the same. She had no idea what he was thinking. She barely knew what she was thinking as she looked at the handsome curves of his face and the generous sweep of his broad shoulders in his tailored black jacket. The ultra-modern restaurant was dimly lit and combined with the dark charcoal and earthy brown tones of the sleek decor it was difficult to make out very much. Except that he was still handsome. So very handsome.

It wasn't cocky good looks he possessed. It was as if he just didn't know how appealing he was to women. He had always been that way. He obviously knew on some level that he was attractive but he never took advantage of it or seemed impressed by the gift nature had bestowed on him. Tom Fielding was a lot deeper than skin alone.

He stood up then hesitated for a moment, as if to

seek some sort of approval to approach. But he did anyway. Her stomach was a tangled mess of nerves as she watched him drop his napkin on the table and cross over to her. His eyes didn't leave her face for an instant.

'Sara,' he began, as he bent down to kiss her cheek. The scent of his cologne filled her senses. It wasn't overpowering, it was subtle and sensual. It was Tom.

'It's so good to see you,' he continued.

Sara was momentarily speechless. She knew she was in Melbourne, it wasn't as if they had bumped into each other in an isolated town on the other side of the world. Perhaps she shouldn't have even been surprised, but it was still overwhelming.

'Lovely to see you too, Tom,' she finally breathed in reply. It was a struggle as she felt her heart cramp.

'May I?' he asked, as his hand rested on the empty chair.

Sara nodded and he pulled out the chair and sat down at her table. Out of habit, he reached across and touched her hand.

Looking back in the harsh light of day, Sara realised that had been her first mistake. She should have kept Tom Fielding at arm's length. It had begun to rain, and Sara regretted not asking her cab from the airport to drop her at the nearest coffee shop to the hospital. She needed a short black to wake herself up after the early flight and couldn't bear the thought of cafeteria coffee. She was in search of the strength only a barista could provide. Picking up her steps even more, her mind raced back to that night. That silly, stupid night four weeks ago.

Dinner alone had turned into dinner for two, then a stroll, and then drinks at a bar in the city. Scars had a way of fading a little in the soft lights of the evening, particularly when wine was involved. Old times, old feelings, old reasons for falling in love replaced the wounds and hurt. Her defences became shaky and, against her will, they finally fell.

Reason didn't have a chance. Just before midnight, they were alone in her hotel room. Tom looked more appealing than any man she had ever seen. Sitting on the edge of her bed in his long black jeans, his suede boots a little dusty, his dark blond hair pushed back in waves that brushed the collar of his white linen shirt. His jacket was flung over the small sofa by the window.

He looked like a cowboy. *Her cowboy for tonight.*

And it could only be for tonight. For old times' sake, she reasoned silently. There was no chance of anything more. They had tried that and it didn't work. She wasn't going there again. She wasn't giving up her dreams for this man. But she knew her heart was finally out of harm's way. It was safely protected inside the walls that she had carefully erected when she had walked out and left him, so she gave in to her desires. It's only one night, she reassured herself.

He was staring straight at her with his bedroom eyes. Despite wondering if she was about to make one of life's bad decisions and one she might just regret, she seemed too powerless to stop herself. Was it lust or was it love? She wasn't sure but it was going to happen.

'Don't tell me to stop, I know what I'm about to do...' she started.

Suddenly her words were cut short by his lips pressing against hers. His hands gently cupped her face as his mouth captured her sigh. She didn't fight him. She didn't want to talk any more. Her hands instinctively reached up and pulled him closer. Her body arched with desire. She was aflame with the heat in his fingers as his hands slid under her clothing to stroke her bare skin. His kisses became more urgent and she opened her mouth to him. She wanted to feel him, to have him, just once more. To feel his body next to hers and to taste him. He unbuttoned her blouse and slid it from her warm skin, tossing it on the floor as he trailed moist kisses down her neck.

'I want you, Sara, and I'm going to have you tonight,' he breathed low and heavy with desire as his fingers traced gentle lines along the bare skin of her thigh.

His hands moved to the curve of her spine and he pulled her even closer to his hard body. She felt her pulse racing as her fingers threaded through his hair and she kissed him more deeply than before. They fell back onto the bed, discarding the last remnants of clothing before their bodies became one.

Sara Fielding had woken in her hotel room the next morning more confused than she thought possible. It had all seemed so clear the night before. Just two people sharing a night of pleasure. Two consenting adults needing each other. Nothing more. But now it was anything but clear. She realised just how vulnerable she still was with Tom. She pulled the sheets up to her chin like a flimsy shield. A feeling of dread hit the pit of her stomach.

As daylight slipped through the gap in the heavy curtains she could see the fine stubble on his chin. The satin sheet was barely covering him, and his tanned chest was sculpted like a statue. They had made love all night and he was still the caring, amazing lover she remembered. But she should never have done it. She looked up at the ceiling of the room, wondering what possessed her to be so stupid and impulsive. It was not like her.

She had spent the last three years trying to push past the hurt and disappointment and then, in a few passionate hours, she had ignored her own logic and risked opening up old wounds. She couldn't blame it on the wine, she hadn't even finished her drink at the restaurant and had hardly touched the martini at the bar.

Hormones, memories, melancholy, maybe even the remnants of the love they had once shared, had overridden the voice of reason and they had returned to her room together.

Now, in the light of morning, she wanted to scream at herself. *Why?*

In a few short weeks he would officially become her ex-husband. The divorce would be finalised. She had managed to stay away for all those years, finally finding the resolve to ask for a divorce, and then, just before it became official, she'd slept with him.

She rolled her eyes in disappointment and confusion. Her lawyer had told her that Tom wasn't contesting the divorce. He had signed the papers. It was just a matter of legal processes being completed.

Perhaps it was knowing that the divorce would be finalised that made her feel safe. That was crazy, she knew, but it was the only explanation she could muster. The divorce was a piece of paper. It wasn't a shield. It couldn't protect her heart.

Tom began to stir. She closed her eyes and feigned sleep. She wasn't sure what to say. Was it *Thank you for a lovely evening* or *I know we slept together but just so you know, I'm not in love with you any more?*

She needed time. Perhaps he would wake up and leave. She felt her stomach knot, not unlike the night before when he'd walked towards her at the restaurant. All those old feelings, the good and the bad, were sitting heavily in her chest.

She wasn't sure if she had imagined it, but as she'd been falling asleep in Tom's arms the night before, she thought she had heard him whisper, *I love you.* She didn't want to go there. She wasn't about to get involved with Tom again. It would be too easy to fall back into his arms. She had taken so long to not need him in her life. To finally realise that she had a right to live her life the way she wanted, whatever it might cost her.

She lay as still as she could. Her breathing was light but laboured as her nerves played with her anxiety level. Last night they had given in to the chemistry they had always shared. But their differences were still there. That hadn't changed and they would never be able to move past what had torn them apart. Sara watched Tom slip from the bed and collect his clothes from all over the room. She wondered if he felt the same. A little part wished he had tried to wake her, to hold her and to talk through their differences. To solve the issues they had and to make love again.

Reason reminded her that it would never happen, so leaving without a word would be best. She hoped he'd leave a note on the hotel stationery. That's all she should expect. All she wanted, she tried to convince herself.

She had loved every minute of his hands and his body on hers. The tenderness and sense of belonging had been undeniable but now, hearing him dressing in the other room, she knew it had been wrong. It had been a lapse in judgement for both of them.

The door of the bathroom opened and Tom emerged fully dressed. Sara closed her eyes again. She didn't want him to catch her awake, thinking about what might have been. He fumbled for his boots then slipped on his jacket. She watched through half-open eyes as he made his way to the desk and scribbled something on the hotel notepad. Quietly, he crossed to the door of her room, opened it and left quietly. He was gone.

As the door shut, Sara sat bolt upright. She was so grateful he was gone. *Or was she?* She felt horribly confused. There was nothing sweeter than falling asleep wrapped in Tom's arms, the heat of his naked body pressed against hers.

But she had to move on. He wouldn't change. He couldn't change. And she was tired of changing for everyone else. She almost had the divorce. She would be free. They would be free of each other. They were two very different people with very different priorities.

She wanted children.

He didn't.

And this time she was walking away to live her life, her way.

She remembered climbing from the warm bed and heading to the shower. Trying to make sense of the night was pointless, she decided as the warm water ran over her back and shoulders. Images of Tom making love to her came rushing back. She closed her eyes and turned to face the water head-on. The water soaked her hair and ran down her face. She was leaving for Texas in eight short weeks. And she would never see Tom Fielding again.

She turned off the water and wrapped herself in a fluffy white bath towel and returned to the scene of the crime. There was a wrapper or two that she didn't want the hotel staff to find, so she picked them up and put them in the bin. Tom was so very good at being bad but he was always very careful.

She crossed to the desk and picked up the note.

Dear Sara,
Lovely to spend time with you. All the very best for Texas.
Always,
Tom x

She smiled, a bittersweet smile at the sadness of the situation. Two people who loved each other but who both had to accept it could never be.

Sara hadn't really pushed for divorce at first but now, with a new life in America awaiting her, she no longer wanted to be Dr Sara Fielding, wife of Dr Tom Fielding. She needed to be single. To have a chance at happiness and a family.

She had only filed for the divorce six months before. She had held onto the idea he would change his mind for too long and she knew it. But Tom had finally agreed to sign the papers. He too had accepted they were over. The way he'd left this morning showed that. Last night had been like two friends who had given in to their emotions for just one night. But her rationale was fragile in the early morning light.

The sudden sound of an ambulance siren brought Sara back from her reverie. She was beside the tall red-brick hospital walls of Augustine General Hospital and quite close to the front doors and the hospital office of her good friend Stu Anderson. Just after she'd returned from her first trip to Melbourne, Stu had mentioned he was in need of a locum oral surgeon to oversee his private practice while he was away. Sara had had the time and had wanted to help out so she had agreed to work the four weeks before she left for the US.

She was aware returning to Melbourne could hold some difficulties but she also knew she had to push past the hurt and accept the shortfalls of the city. The shortfalls being her failed marriage and the sadness that weighed down her memories of the time she had spent there. She'd studied, she'd fallen in love and she'd left. Now, all these years later she thought she needed to accept that life wasn't perfect here but she didn't need to stay away any longer. She just needed to keep her emotions in check.

With this new resolve, it hadn't seemed such a bad idea when she had agreed to help out but now, being back in the city, memories of the night she had spent with Tom came charging back, and she was a little more anxious about her stay.

She tried to remind herself that Melbourne was a big city. She could avoid the Vue de Monde, and the martini bar. That wouldn't be too difficult as there were many more restaurants and she wasn't that fond of vermouth anyway. And luckily Tom consulted at a hospital the other side of the city.

Mindful of the hospital traffic, Sara kept to the pedestrian pathway as she made her way to the entrance. The ambulance had pulled up in the emergency parking bay and the paramedics, now joined by two hospital staff, were already removing the gurney from the back of the vehicle.

She walked around to the automatic sliding doors of the visitors' entrance. At least she was finally under shelter. Removing her heavy overcoat, she shook the excess water out over the large grey rubber mat before she placed the coat over her arm and stepped inside. Thankfully, inside the hospital was much warmer than outside. She slipped off her gloves and placed them into the pocket of her coat. Crossing to the information counter, she ran her fingers through her damp hair and wiped the moisture from her face.

'Hello, I'm here to see Dr Anderson. Oral maxillofacial surgery.'

The receptionist smiled, although the second glances Sara was receiving from the other administration staff made her think her appearance was a little battered by the weather. She quickly realised her hair was more than just damp when she felt trickles run down her temples and into her left ear.

The young woman picked up a box of tissues from behind the high grey and white panelled counter and offered them to Sara. 'It's really coming down out there, isn't it?'

With an embarrassed smile she took a few tissues and mopped her wet forehead, cheeks and ear.

'You need to take the elevator at the end of this corridor up to the fourth floor and you'll find the oral surgery consulting rooms on the left as you step out.'

'Thanks,' Sara replied, trying to stifle a yawn. The effect of a long night of surgery, combined with an early morning flight, was starting to show. Sara had tried to keep busy since her last trip to Melbourne; she hadn't wanted any time to think about what she had done. Unfortunately, returning to Melbourne was rapidly bringing it all back.

Tom Fielding sat in his office on the fourth floor of Augustine General Hospital, thinking back to the night he'd spent with Sara, the way he had thought about it every day for the last four weeks. Each day since that fateful night vivid, unwanted memories had reminded him of how much he still loved his soon-to-be-ex-wife. Still wanted her but couldn't have her. He had decided to give her the divorce, hand her back her life and return to his alone. But that one night together had destroyed the solace he had finally found; it ate away at his core that there was no future for them. They had different goals, different plans for their lives, and there was no common ground any more.

Except in a hotel room at midnight.

Tom remembered his surprise and elation when he'd spied his beautiful ex-wife sitting alone across from him in the restaurant. In his eyes she was still the most gorgeous, captivating woman in the world. She was intelligent, kind, caring, strong willed and the most giving lover a man could want. A shared dinner had led to drinks and then to her hotel.

Once he had been inside her room, Tom hadn't been able to control himself any longer. Sara had made it very clear that she wanted him just as much. He had been risking everything, including his sanity, but he'd wanted this woman more than life itself. Even if it was for just one last time.

In the morning Tom had opened his eyes to see his wife lying beside him. Ex-wife, reasoning reminded him. She was sleeping so soundly. She was so beautiful. Her short blonde hair had been a mess, a beautiful mess. A mess he had created when he'd been making love to her all night. The curves of her naked body had been softly lit by the rays that had peeped through the curtain break.

He'd resisted the urge to stroke her soft, tempting skin. She was such a sound sleeper, he knew that from the time they'd spent as husband and wife, but he hadn't wanted to risk waking her. He'd known he had to slip from the bed and leave. It would be best for both of them. Trying to make sense of what they'd done would be impossible. Sara had made it very clear that she was heading overseas. She was starting a new life and he had to do the same. He had to give her the divorce. He had to give her the freedom she needed and return to his life without her.

He loved her, and maybe she still loved him a little at least, but in a few weeks they would be divorced. She had reminded him of that fact last night in the restaurant. She was moving on, she had told him at the bar where they'd enjoyed a martini together. Leaving for the US in a few weeks to start afresh in a new country, she had told him at the door of her hotel room at midnight.

They hadn't talked about their past, they hadn't talked about their work. And they hadn't spoken about their differences. They'd spoken about the present, about light-hearted subjects. It was as if they had been two strangers who hadn't wanted to know anything too deep about each other.

It was an unspoken agreement; each knowing they would only share one last night. Tom didn't want to hold up his end of that unspoken agreement. He wanted his wife back. He wanted to wake up every morning with her in his arms. But he was a logical man and he accepted that could never be.

Before he'd left the room he had paused to take one last look at Sara still asleep in the rumpled bed sheets. She'd looked like an angel. *His angel for one last night.*

CHAPTER TWO

'SLOW DOWN...AND tell me how exactly you came to misplace a patient?'

'I'm not sure, Dr Fielding. His name was...oh, what was his name again? That's right...Kowalski...Joseph Kowalski. I can't believe he's gone. I messed up big time. I'm so sorry, Dr Fielding. I'm really sorry. I'm such an idiot.'

'Johnson, take a breath. I examined Mr Kowalski in my ward a little over an hour ago. He had multiple mandibular fractures and if I'm not mistaken a blood alcohol close to point two. He was in a hospital gown and hooked up to an IV. I can't see him travelling very far without being noticed.'

Sara Fielding stepped back from the open doorway to where she couldn't be seen. *Dr Fielding?* What was he doing here? He didn't consult at this hospital. He was the oral and maxillofacial consultant at Lower North Eastern on the other side of the city. It was where she had done her training. It was where they met. Why was he here? He must be visiting Stu to say goodbye, as they were friends. They had all been friends once, she reminded herself.

'I know, right, how far could he get?' the young voice returned in varying pitch, trying to convince himself of a good outcome. But his struggle showed when his voice gave in to a nervous stutter. 'I—I spoke with Security at the b-back and front gates and he hasn't left the grounds.'

'Well, that's comforting, I'd hate to see footage of our escapee on television tonight. We don't want to see our director's face on the six p.m. news if they splash shots of the bare backside of an inebriated elderly man, still attached to an IV stand, walking down Swan Street. I can only imagine the paperwork involved with that Ministerial inquiry.'

Stunned, Sara collapsed back against the wall out of the view of Tom and the young man she assumed was either a final year undergraduate or an intern. *Our director?* Her heart was racing and her stomach had tied itself in a knot. She didn't hear any of what he was telling the young man after those two words, she just heard the thumping of the blood in her temples. Tom Fielding must now be consulting at this hospital. *Her hospital.*

'Security, please.' Tom spoke into the phone then, while waiting for the connection, he began skimming through the unread emails on his computer screen. After a moment, he continued. 'It's Tom Fielding, I'm just checking on the status of a missing patient. Joseph Kowalski. Admitted to the oral surgery ward about two hours ago, apparently did a runner out of the ward... Oh, okay. The cafeteria—poor man's probably hungry. So where is he now? Right, that's unfortunate. I'll send the intern to collect him promptly. Thanks.' With that he hung up the phone.

'Well, Johnson, I suggest you head to the florist on the ground floor. Kowalski's in there, trying to purchase a bouquet, and apparently while searching for his imaginary wallet underneath his hospital gown he has managed to show the family jewels to the volunteers. They're a little disturbed, so you need to calmly head down and collect him. But remember, you're no good to anyone, and particularly not Mr Kowalski, if you beat yourself up about it. You followed hospital procedure. You notified Security, and me, and they have him. Good outcome, so just head off and take him back to the ward pronto.'

Sara clenched her eyes closed. Her mind was struggling to process what was happening. It made no sense to her. Stu had set up the appointment at the hospital to discuss his caseload and show her around the operating theatres. Then he was going to take her to his practice, which was apparently only a few blocks away. There had definitely been no mention of Tom in the conversation. If there had been she wouldn't have agreed to come. Nervously, she smoothed her skirt and tugged her jacket back into position.

More than anything, she wanted to run. To disappear and not face Tom again. But she couldn't. She had made a promise to Stu to locum for him for the month. A promise she couldn't break.

The heat began rising in her cheeks. Her heart began beating a little faster. Elevating anxiety was threatening her composure but she was fighting back. She tried to put the situation into perspective quickly. She had limited time to find a solution, a tidy way to process this.

The practice would occupy most of her time. There would be Theatre two days a week or perhaps only one and a half. She would be consulting at the private practice at least three days, maybe even three and a half. Thoughts of their recent night together, their romantic whirlwind engagement and their year as husband and wife had to be replaced hurriedly with a professional demeanour. She needed to rebuild those walls that had protected her for the last three years and which would once again be her saviour when she walked into the office to face Tom.

Clearly his presence at the hospital would complicate things but she wouldn't run and hide. She needed to face this head-on. She was thirty-two years old now with a respected medical career. The fact that they had spent one crazy night together couldn't affect their work, they had to put it behind them.

Perhaps he already had done that, she told herself. He had left the hotel room without a word and he hadn't contacted her since, so he must be feeling the same way. She desperately needed to freeze her heart before she saw his face.

Reaching down for her briefcase, she waited a moment for the young man to leave. With her head held high, she would walk into Tom's office and behave as if nothing had ever happened.

Unfortunately, she assumed the young man would be walking, not running, and not straight into her.

His full weight met with her tiny frame, sending her crashing back into the wall and her briefcase tumbling down to the ground.

'Oh, no, I'm so sorry. I didn't see you there,' he gasped, as he reached out to steady Sara. 'Are you okay?'

Sara was stunned into silence for a moment. Finally she managed to mutter, 'I'm fine, really.' She was a little shaken but didn't want to make a fuss. Bending down to gather her belongings, she didn't think the day could get any worse.

'No, you're not. You're bleeding. You've cut your leg!'

Sara spied the gash on her knee. The open lock on her briefcase must have cut her before it hit the ground.

'Come with me. You'll have to sit down while I get some antiseptic and gauze.' The young man directed Sara into the office he had just left. Tom's office. This was not the entrance she had hoped to make, which had been walking in confidently and meeting Tom on an equal footing. Now, limping in, she wasn't going to meet him on any footing.

Tom didn't lift his eyes from the papers he was reading on his desk. Sara noticed his white exam coat was still thrown over the chair. He had always hated wearing it, and apparently he still did. The top button of his blue striped shirt was undone and there was no sign of a tie.

'They're waiting downstairs, Johnson…you need to get there stat.' His voice was stern but not abrasive.

Sara stood in the doorway supported by her apologetic assailant. Across the room she watched the man who had captured her heart all those years ago and who had made love to her only a few short weeks ago. For the briefest moment time seemed to stand still. Her resolve to forget their history vanished and she found herself wondering how it would be if things had been different between them.

She hated feeling this way. It wasn't fair and she couldn't allow her feelings to cloud her future. The chemistry they shared had allowed the anger and frustration to dissipate over dinner and drinks. But here in the hospital she would fight it. Her biological clock was ticking louder than her heart and she was determined that Tom Fielding would not rob her of the chance to have a family. She would not make that sacrifice. Letting him leave the hotel room had proved to Sara that she had the reserves to do it. To walk away a second time, and to let him do the same.

Tom's eyes were shadowed by a slight frown before he lifted his head and met her gaze. Abruptly the frown vanished and he stood to his feet.

'Sara, I thought you were in San Antonio. What are you doing here?' Suddenly Tom's eyes dropped to the injury on her leg. 'Are you hurt? What on earth happened?' Concern etched his voice as he crossed the room with long purposeful strides. He drew her into his arms and pulled her close to his firm body as Johnson released his support.

Sara resisted Tom's hold. She tried to pull away but his strong arms held her still.

'I crashed into her, Dr Fielding. I didn't see her. I'm sorry. She was waiting outside but I was in a hurry and *boof*—I hit her.' The young man re-enacted the collision with his hands.

'Grab that chair,' Tom said, motioning towards the large armchair that sat by the window. 'Bring it here quickly.'

The young man dragged the chair across the room and Tom gently lowered Sara onto the cushioned leather.

'There's a first-aid kit in the cupboard to the right of the bookcase.'

Sara heard the instructions Tom gave to Johnson but her eyes were transfixed on Tom as he crossed the room to retrieve a small footstool by the bookcase.

He looked every bit as gorgeous in the daylight as he had that night just a month ago. His lean, angular face was slightly tanned and his grey eyes were luminous beneath his sandy brows.

He smiled at her as he carried the footstool back, his

wide sensual mouth slowly curving upwards. But she would not reciprocate.

Tom had no place in her life any more. In fact, he should never have been there. They were two very different people with completely different priorities in life.

Sara swallowed hard. 'It's just a little scratch, honestly. It's nothing…' Her words were cut short when she felt the warmth of his hands on her bare skin. He looked into her eyes as he knelt on the floor beside her, gently lifting her leg and placing it on the stool. He moved the hem of her skirt slightly to assess the damage to her knee. She swallowed hard. She hated that the feel of his fingers lightly touching her skin sent shivers down her spine. Again she wished she had worn heavy woollen tights, but this time it wasn't because of the cold.

Johnson handed him an antiseptic wipe and some gauze.

'It's just a superficial wound. I'll clean it up but I think a plaster will suffice.'

'I'm so glad and I'm so sorry, I mean it. I can't believe what a day I've had and now this—'

'We'll be fine here, Johnson,' Tom interrupted. 'Go and collect your patient but this time just take it a little slower.'

'Are you sure? You don't need anything?'

'Positive,' Tom replied, not taking his eyes off Sara.

Sara watched from the corner of her eye as the young man put the first-aid kit back on Tom's desk, picked up her briefcase and overcoat from the doorway, put them by her chair and left the room.

And left them alone.

Tom's hands were still cradling her leg. The plaster was securely attached to the clean wound but he didn't want to release her. He had forgotten how good it felt to have Sara this close. He had no idea why she was in his office but for the briefest moment he didn't care. She was with him again. Near him again. And he could touch her soft, warm skin. Her perfume was invading his senses. It was the same fragrance she had always worn. So little had changed and yet so much had changed for ever.

Finally he came to his senses and reluctantly released his hold, standing up and moving back to his desk. He looked at the woman before him. She was as beautiful as the day they'd met, the day they'd married and the day she'd left him. But she *had* left him.

'What brings you back to Melbourne and my office?' he asked, as he rested back against the wooden frame and folded his arms across his chest. 'I thought you'd be in Texas by now.' He suddenly felt the need to protect himself. Then the realisation of why she had come to the hospital hit him. She must have grown tired of waiting for the divorce papers to make the return trip to her, so she had made the visit to collect them herself.

'The documents are with my lawyer. No doubt they'll be with yours tomorrow.'

Sara suddenly realised that Tom had no idea either. He was obviously equally clueless that they would be working at the same hospital.

'I'm not here for the papers, Tom. Although I'm glad to hear that's progressing,' she announced. 'No, actually, I'm here to work for a month, filling in for Stu.'

'You're filling in for Stu?' Tom was gobsmacked.

'You never said anything that night when we...' He hesitated for a minute. He didn't want to allude to what he knew they were both thinking. He cleared his throat. 'When we bumped into each other. I'm surprised you didn't say anything.'

Sara just stared at him for a moment, trying desperately to push the vivid snapshots of the evening from her mind.

'I didn't know back then, when we…' She paused. It was becoming more awkward and uncomfortable by the minute. 'That night, well, I hadn't spoken with Stu and I had no idea you consulted here. But even if I had known, if you remember, we didn't talk work at all.'

Tom nodded in silence.

Sara knew she would never have accepted Stu's proposal to fill in for him if she had known Tom worked at the hospital where she would be operating. She had assumed he was safely ensconced at the other side of town. But she had to deal with the situation. There was no other choice. Stu would never find another oral surgeon on short notice and she would never leave him high and dry like that. She just had to deal with Tom.

'So, what are you doing at this hospital?'

'I'm the associate professor of oral surgery.'

Sara was taken aback. Tom hadn't said a word that night. With a title like that, and the extraordinary workload and dedication to achieve such a position, he had certainly earned some bragging rights. But he had said nothing about it. She wanted to say how proud she was of him, but of course pride carried ownership or at the very least attachment, and she couldn't afford either.

'Congratulations, Tom,' she finally decided, keeping it simple. 'That must have been a lot of work. You must be the youngest associate professor on staff.'

'So they say. But I'd completed my PhD, and had a year post-doctoral experience so I met the selection criteria. The board approved my appointment for three years and I'm only six months into it,' he responded. The PhD had kept his mind from missing Sara after she left. It had provided him with a focus and purpose in getting up each day.

'I still operate on private patients but I'm more involved with the teaching and rotation programme in the undergraduate, graduate and professional curricula and the development of post-qualifying modules. But enough about me. I'm still in shock that you are Stu's mysterious replacement.'

'What do you mean, mysterious?' Sara replied, giving him a puzzled look.

'I mean he hadn't told me who was filling in at the practice. Stu told me that he had it covered but not that you were his replacement.'

Sara was even more confused. Stu's private practice was not his concern. 'Why do you discuss his practice? Don't you still have your own?'

Tom gave her a wry look. 'Because we're partners, Stu's a partner now in my old practice—he bought in a few months ago. I only consult there one day a week now. The hospital consumes most of my time, but I still wanted to maintain some patient contact.'

Sara was completely flustered for a moment. Not only was Tom consulting at the hospital where she would be operating but he was also a partner at the practice where she would be consulting for the next month. She would be working at Tom's old practice. This was quickly spiralling into a disaster.

'Oh, well, at least this will be uncomfortable for both of us,' she said honestly.

Tom stood watching her carefully, looking for clues as to what she was thinking and, more importantly, feeling. He wanted some signs that would let him into her head. There was nothing. She really had shut him out. That night had been nothing but a moment of passion between two lonely people in a big city. Nothing more.

He knew then and there what he had to do. He had to keep his ex-wife away from his heart. Or he'd go mad. It was crazy and he knew it but he still loved the woman sitting there, so close but emotionally so distant. The woman who had captured his heart all those years ago still held it quite firmly in her hands. He had to push her away. Or, more to the point, he had to push her out of his reach.

He didn't need a reminder of why she'd left. Or why she'd had to leave. They had shared that discussion too many times to recall.

Any feelings she'd once had for him were clearly gone. He had to accept it. And so he adopted the same detached demeanour. A demeanour very far from his true feelings.

'There really shouldn't be any problems. That night...' He paused. 'Let's just say old habits, reminiscing, we crossed the line, both of us. It won't happen again. But, hey, we got it out of our systems. Like an itch that needed a good scratch, and now it's done we can both move on.'

Sara was thrown by his response. It was cold. He really was over them. An *itch*? That sounded so unlike the Tom she had known. Still, three years had passed and he had obviously changed. Or, just like her, was he putting on a façade to make the arrangement they found themselves in a little less awkward? It didn't matter. They both knew and understood the rules.

Without answering, Tom crossed back to her and reached for her leg. Sara jumped as his hand gently lifted her leg down from the stool and placed her foot back on the floor.

'We're good, Sara...we're good.'

* * *

Sara wasn't so sure. She was going to be operating at the hospital for a month. That meant bumping into each other, on ward rounds, near the OR. There were too many opportunities where they would see each other.

The way her body had reacted to Tom made her realise only too quickly that the chemistry she shared with him wasn't just a memory. She suddenly worried if her love for him would ever truly be over. But they had no future. She would not give up on the idea of bringing children into the world. Being a mother was a dream she wanted to hold onto but Tom never wanted to be a father. That was written in stone.

She had spent too long getting him out of her head and her heart.

Sara looked at him, and even through her tired eyes she could see the man who won her love was still as handsome and charismatic as ever. *It's four short weeks. It can't be that difficult.*

'I'm a little tired—can we discuss the work schedule later? We can sort out the personal arrangements too over the next few days. I'm happy with the financial separation the way it is. It won't change after we divorce. You won't need to support me, so it should be done very quickly.'

There was an uncomfortable silence between them. She had no idea what was going on in Tom's mind but he clearly wasn't about to share anything. She had said her piece and cleared the air.

'Quick and painless, like an extraction of an upper molar,' he said matter-of-factly.

Sara knew when Tom became uncomfortable he always used dark humour. It was how he masked his emotions.

'Not quite,' she replied, then chose to change the subject. 'After the four weeks here, I'm off. I don't know a lot about Texas but the position sounded exciting and I jumped at it,' she told him as she crossed to one of the floor-to-ceiling bookcases that lined the room. Part of her didn't want to go to the US. Part of her still wanted Tom. But she also wanted more.

Sara lightly ran her fingers over a row of leather-bound medical books standing next to one another on the shelf and thought back to all of the nights she had spent poring over books just like them as a postgraduate student at the university library, hoping to come close to Tom's knowledge and skill. But it wasn't just his ability and compassion as a doctor that had her in awe, it was his commanding presence as a man that had drawn her to him. He had been her lecturer and her mentor but more than that, she had wished he was her lover.

She had felt on some level there was chemistry that ran between them. She would watch him standing at the lectern, speaking to all the medical students, and she had hoped, as his eyes had scanned the lecture hall, that he had seen her as more than just his student. She had wanted him to see her as a woman. A woman who respected his knowledge, admired his skills but wanted to know more about him as a man.

Sara would daydream in the tram on the way home, a bag full of handwritten notes at her feet and a laptop in her backpack, about the two of them driving home together. She had pictured them talking about their days, comparing notes on cases and discussing surgical procedures. Sara remembered back to the long nights when she would lie in twisted sheets staring at the ceiling in the darkness of her university bedroom. She would picture the curves of his handsome face, the skin wrinkling softly around his grey eyes when he laughed, and the warm, masculine scent of his body.

Not being able to say how she felt during those many months of study was at times almost impossible. But she knew better than to say anything to her incredibly handsome tutor. It was more than likely that her romantic musings were one-sided. She didn't want her imagination to steer her into attracting more of his attention. He was almost seven years older, infinitely wiser and often intimidating. And she was his student. Capable and willing to learn, passing with distinctions, but still his student.

She thought he would be more interested in dating one of his peers, yet there were moments when she felt there was something more. She would ask a question, or answer one that he had posed, and he would appear genuinely impressed.

There were times when his eyes seemed to linger on her a little longer. His mouth would curve ever so slightly and his eyes seemed to be smiling. Her heart would skip a beat, and she hoped she didn't blush. Sometimes he would ask her to stay late with a small number of postgraduates to discuss a topic or alternate prognosis in greater depths. On more than one occasion he bumped into her in the university cafeteria and they shared a table and talked of things other than work.

She wanted more than anything for his interest to be more than just academic, and these chats led her to believe it was, but he was a complicated man. She decided that until her training was over and he made his feelings clear she would keep her own locked safely inside her heart.

Sara never regretted that decision. Soon after she graduated and found a role in a private practice based in Brighton, Tom invited her to a celebratory dinner. She was so surprised and happy. It was a dinner for two. Standing at the door of the restaurant as they waited for their table, his soft hands cupped her face and gently turned her towards him. Tenderly, he reached down and kissed her.

It took Sara's breath away. Her intuition about his feelings had been right all along. The man of her dreams, of all her late-night fantasies, was kissing her. And not caring who saw them.

She remembered every wonderful warm feeling that rushed through her body when, with love in his eyes and a wicked grin, he whispered huskily that given the chance he would never let her out of his sight again. He told her he wanted to keep her in his arms for ever.

It was a whirlwind romance. Every second weekend they spent away at different cosy bed and breakfasts all over Victoria and then, three months after their first date, Tom surprised Sara with a trip to Paris. Winter had set in and they had planned on heading to the ski slopes of Mount Hotham. The night before they were due to leave for the snow, sitting by the heater in Sara's apartment eating raisin toast and sipping on hot chocolate, Tom told Sara there was a slight change in plans but one he hoped she would like. He suggested that she should pack some summer clothes and her passport instead of thermal underwear. As Sara frantically emptied her suitcase of her sweaters, ski pants and thick socks, hurriedly replacing them with cotton dresses, shorts and T-shirts, she told him that he was crazy.

And he told her that he loved her.

Tom managed to keep the new holiday destination a secret until the cab arrived at Tullamarine airport and he carried their luggage to the Air France check-in. Sara was so excited that she felt her eyes brimming with tears as she took her boarding pass, destination Paris.

Together, they spent a blissful week at Hotel Mansart on Paris's Right Bank. They strolled hand in hand around the Tuileries Garden and along the pathways lined with tulips. Tom was the most romantic, wonderful lover and Sara knew without doubt that she was totally and completely in love. She couldn't help but smile with happiness as they sat together by the sparkling pools in the warmth of a perfect summer day. A perfect day with her perfect man and Sara thought life couldn't be any more wonderful.

But it could. And a short time later it did. As they stood admiring the Maillol sculptures in the soft light of sunset, Tom fell to one knee and slipped a diamond solitaire ring on Sara's finger. She gasped and nodded before she kissed the man of her dreams and fell into his arms. She knew with all of her heart it was where she belonged.

After years of study to qualify as an oral and maxillofacial surgeon, Sara was twenty-eight years of age and Tom was about to turn thirty-five so they decided to have a very short engagement and that night as they lay in each other's arms they set a wedding date only three months away.

Sara was going to spend her life with a man she completely and utterly adored and she had never been so happy in her life…

'Sara. Yoo-hoo, I asked you when exactly you're leaving for cattle country?'

CHAPTER THREE

SARA RAISED HER chin and turned around to face Tom. She looked across the room to see him sitting back down in his high-backed leather chair. She thanked the heavens that, no matter how extraordinarily talented her estranged husband was, at least he wasn't a mind-reader.

She was angry with herself for the way she was reacting to him again. She was so distracted. Closing her eyes for a moment, she took a deep, calming breath. She had to get her emotions under control. Tom was bringing back feelings that she couldn't afford to entertain. She had other plans.

But now, seeing Tom again, her heart began questioning her head.

Would she ever find a man she loved as much as Tom?

She had dated a few men over the past three years but not one of them had ever matched up. She always compared her dates to Tom. She hated that she did it. And she hated that they never came close.

She cursed silently as she studied him. He wasn't going to ruin her life. She could be happy one day and have the big messy family that she'd always wanted. She deserved a man in her life who was willing to give her that family.

'Listen, Tom, I think that it's best I head to the hotel and put my feet up for a while.'

There was a knock on the door, forcing Sara to step back. A tall, well-dressed woman entered, a clipboard in hand. She was very attractive and Sara guessed her to be in her late twenties. Her hair was short and dark in a Cleopatra cut, which suited her almond shaped eyes and Mediterranean features.

'Tom, I'm sorry to interrupt but I thought you should know that tomorrow afternoon's list has an alteration. The mandibular advancement, Troy Reeves, has cancelled. Influenza. I've rescheduled him for the twentieth of the month. With any luck you'll finish surgery by six tomorrow night.'

'Christina, this is Sara,' Tom said, as he reached for the amended list. 'Sara, this is Christina, my secretary.'

Both women smiled courteously.

'Christina, if you've done your bit, go on home,' Tom told her. 'I really appreciate you coming in on a weekend. I'll make it up to you.'

'Don't be silly, Tom. I'm happy to help out under the circumstances and I'll see you around seven.' With that she headed back to the open door. 'Nice to meet you, Sara.'

Sara smiled and with equal grace said goodbye before the door closed.

'Don't know what I'd do without her,' Tom remarked casually. 'She's a remarkable woman.'

Sara felt an unexpected ache in her heart when she heard him talk that way about another woman. And they had plans at seven. They had a date. It was ridiculous to be feeling anything other than elation. But she didn't. She felt jealous. It was insane. Why should she care what he thought of or, for that matter, did with other women? Tom could date other women. And now he'd signed the divorce papers he could marry another woman. *As long as she didn't want children.* It wasn't her concern what he did.

You wanted a divorce and now you have it within your reach. And don't forget it, she reminded herself as she tried to pull her thoughts back to the situation at hand.

Before Sara had a chance to open her mouth, the door burst open again. She spun around and found herself being hauled into the arms of a tall, rather robust man with a bushy beard. She felt dwarfed by his stature. He hugged her ferociously and then stepped back.

Sara had to steady herself. It took a moment for her to register just who was on the giving end of the exuberant embrace.

'Sara,' he said. 'You're looking great. How long has it been?'

'Stuart!' she managed to return, realising it was her old friend hiding beneath the thick facial hair. His trademark mop of russet curls hadn't changed at all, now she took stock of him, neither had his twinkling brown eyes in rimless glasses. 'Gosh, it must be three years or more. Last time I saw you would've been…at…um…your…' She stumbled over her words.

A cough echoed from across the room. 'I think Sara's trying to say it was at your anniversary party just before we went our different ways,' Tom interjected. 'And by the way, Stu, it would've been nice of you to let me in on the fact Sara was filling in for you. I had no idea.'

Stuart just shrugged his shoulders. 'Should've read the memo I left on your desk in the office.'

'Maybe you should have just told me.'

'I'm not your secretary, Dr Fielding. We're partners!'

Sara smiled at the banter. They were like bickering children.

'It's lovely to see you again, Stu,' she cut in, to change the subject before it escalated further.

'Just wonderful to see you, gorgeous. You haven't changed a bit. Stunning as always,' he said, stepping back. 'I'm sorry I was delayed in ICU. I wanted to be here when you arrived and talk through everything but since Tom is here I'm sure he can run you through my caseload and his as well. He's going to take over my day at the hospital and you will cover his day there. It's easier than trying to have you cover at the hospital for me. Way too much paperwork in this place,' he said, rolling his eyes.

'Okay, I'm happy to fit in where I can,' Sara said after hearing the update. She'd had no idea she would be covering for anyone else, let alone Tom, but it did make sense.

'I'm glad I got to thank you in person before I leave. You're a trouper. Dana and I can't tell you how much it means to us.'

'It's my pleasure. Are you looking forward to your time off?'

'It's not exactly time off for the sake of it. I'm taking time out to be with Bonny. She was hurt in an accident up on the farm. The tractor lost its grip on an embankment. It rolled into a ditch where Bonny was playing.'

'Oh, my...' Sara's hand instinctively covered her mouth. 'When did that happen?'

'A few weeks back. She's okay. She's out of hospital now. I mean, all things considered, she's doing really well. It was a dirty great tractor and she's so tiny and it could have been much worse. Thankfully there were huge great boulders that took the full weight of the tractor. It fell sideways and Bonny got injured when the metal toolbox lost its moorings and landed on her. She was knocked unconscious and her leg was pinned underneath the exhaust pipe.' The pain in his eyes couldn't mask the distress he was feeling at retelling the story.

Sara was horrified at the thought of Bonny pinned beneath the tractor. She felt her own spine rush with cold and then tears begin to build. She blinked them away.

'I didn't want to guilt you into coming so I didn't mention Bonny when you offered to fill in. It would've been unfair to put that sort of pressure on you.'

'It wouldn't have been pressure. You know I would do anything for you and Dana. I'm just so incredibly sorry to hear about all of this,' Sara told him truthfully. 'I'm glad I'm here, and I hope you can just focus on Bonny and get her better even sooner.'

'She's up and walking but still in a frame,' Stuart told her. 'But she's determined to get back on those little feet of hers. I know she can do it and I think she's going to get better that much sooner with me home full time to help her through the physio. I'm usually home three days a week then here in Melbourne, consulting, the other four.'

Sara watched as Stuart looked pensively down toward his hands and nervously twisted his wedding band back and forth. She felt helpless to ease the almost tangible pain he was suffering.

'She hasn't regained her speech yet,' he began, in little more than a dying whisper.

Sara reached for his hands and encircled them in her own.

'If she's anything like you, little Bonny will be back on her feet and telling you off before you know it.'

He coughed to clear his throat and slowly pulled his hands free of hers and stepped away from her. Sara suspected it was some sort of male strategy he was using to keep his emotions in check.

'I know she will. It's Dana that needs convincing. The specialists have told us with family around her full time she'll be racing ahead. I originally organised a nurse to help out with the twins so Dana could spend time with Bonny, but now, thanks to you taking over for the next month, we can keep it just the family and I know it will make all the difference to her recovery.'

Stuart wrapped one arm around her shoulder and pulled her close again in a bear hug. 'Dana sends her love and hopes you can visit us at the farm soon. We've had it for two years now. Dana really wants you to meet the twins. They're nearly one and, of course, Bonny's almost seven now.'

Sara felt a twinge of guilt for not returning to Melbourne to visit Stuart and Dana. The four of them had shared some wonderful times together, but after the separation Sara had felt the need to stay away from risk of seeing Tom. She'd emailed often and called occasionally. She'd sent them a basket filled with toys and baby gifts when the twins were born. But for the last few months she had been too focused on planning the trip and hadn't spoken to them. Obviously because of the accident and their priority being Bonny, they hadn't reached out to her either.

'It has been far too long since I saw you,' she began. 'I really would love to visit you and Dana on the farm when Bonny is up to it.'

'Of course, Dana would love it,' he responded. 'Sars, some things never change, you know, like you and Tom. Good friends you can always rely on in times of need.'

Sara was having trouble concentrating. Her mind was spinning with images of helpless little Bonny lying in the ditch beneath the tractor. She could only imagine how devastating it had been for the family.

She was deep in terrible, vivid thoughts she didn't want to have filling her head, when Stuart's prickly beard brushed against her neck as he kissed her cheek to thank her yet again.

'I won't forget this, kiddo,' Stuart told her. 'If there's ever anything I can ever do for you, just ask.'

'Don't you think twice about it,' she returned. 'Just get Bonny well—that's enough for me.'

'Well, I expect to see you up on the farm the first break you get.' He smiled and was gone, leaving her alone in the office with Tom.

The atmosphere in the office changed within moments.

With calm composure Sara walked to the door and softly closed it. Her hand quietly released the handle before she turned on her heel and marched over to his desk. 'Why didn't you tell me about Bonny when we caught up the other night?'

'I hadn't seen you for three years, we were keeping it light and I didn't see the point. You said you were leaving to live in Texas. What could you have done? I had no idea that you were coming here to work with me...'

'Neither did I, but surely something as serious as that would rate a mention.' Sara was angry with Tom and not afraid to let him know it.

'Sara, you walked out on me. You walked out on our life together and everything we shared. You never brought up Stu or Dana that night. What right do you have to question me about my actions or what I do and don't tell you? We shared a few hours together. I don't know what's been happening in your life any more than you know what's been happening in mine. We kept it light, Sara, so don't lecture me about what I should and shouldn't have shared with you.' His lips were tight and his mouth formed a hard line.

Sara stepped back. She was acutely aware that Tom was right. She had walked away and she had no right to criticise him. She hadn't asked about Stu and Dana during the evening they'd spent together. That night she had purposely steered the conversation away from anything and anyone that linked her back to their life together.

'You're right. I'm sorry,' she said, regret tainting her voice. 'I guess it wasn't your job to bring me up to speed that night. It's just that we were so close to Stu and Dana and I wish I'd known. I wish they'd called me or I'd called them.'

Sara realised that she had only herself to blame. It wasn't Tom's fault. Her lack of sleep was finally taking its toll and she could feel that her eyes were becoming heavy.

'Tom, I've had a long night and I need to get some sleep, maybe just a short nap.' She reached for a pen and began writing on a small message pad on his desk. 'This is the name of my hotel. I'll call you in a few hours after I take a nap and perhaps we can sort out the working arrangements for the next month over a late lunch.'

Sara woke to the sound of a knock at her door.

She lifted her head from the pillow, surprised to find the room dark. She sat bolt upright and could see the bright lights of the city skyline through her window. A muted glow from the corridor was creeping under the narrow gap below her door.

Fumbling a little, she reached for the lamp beside

the bed. Her blurry eyes tried to focus on her watch. *It couldn't be. Seven o'clock, in the evening?* She must have slept for almost ten hours. She looked down to find she was still dressed in her suit and lying on top of the bed covers.

'Who is it?' she called out, as she climbed from the bed.

'Tom,' his husky voice returned. 'I thought we'd go out for a late lunch. It's nearly eight here but it has to be lunchtime somewhere in the world. Maybe in Texas they're tucking into buffalo wings.'

Sara smiled but she felt uncomfortable knowing that he was at the door of her hotel room. She remembered only too well what had happened last time.

She ran the brush through her hair once more, quickly looked in the mirror and cleared the smudges of mascara from under her eyes, then crossed the room. Her hands ran over her crinkled skirt and, as respectable as she could look under the circumstances, she opened the door.

Tom stood before her, dressed in a fine grey polo knit and black trousers. His hair was swept back from his forehead in gentle, still-damp waves. He looked as if he had just climbed from the shower. It only took seconds for his subtle cologne to penetrate her senses.

'Hello, Tom,' she managed, glad that her tone was cool, despite how nervous she felt or how handsome he looked, standing in her doorway. 'Just to let you know it's not eight, it's only seven.'

He grinned ruefully. 'No, it's nearly eight, you're on Victorian time now, you're not in Adelaide anymore. You must be tired,' he said, tilting his head to one side. 'Are you up to grabbing a bite to eat?'

She glanced down at her watch. He was right on

both counts. It was eight and she definitely wasn't in Adelaide anymore. She was in Melbourne and she was uncomfortably close to her far too handsome and soon to be ex-husband.

'I suppose I am a little peckish,' she began trying to push away how he was making her feel. She looked down and saw again how crumpled her clothes were after flying and then sleeping in them. 'Can you give me fifteen minutes to freshen up?'

'Not a problem. I'll wait downstairs.' With that he walked off down the corridor to the lift.

She watched him. The way he swayed just slightly as he walked. The way his clothes fit his masculine body. The perfect silhouette of his broad shoulders and slim waist.

'I'll be in the bar,' he called back, turning around too quickly for her to pretend she wasn't watching him.

She slammed the door shut with her foot, angry with herself once again.

The hot water over her body felt good and she wished she could stay there longer but she knew she had to get downstairs. Quickly, she applied light make-up and then searched through her suitcase for something that didn't need ironing.

She chose a salmon knitted top and cream slacks, casually draping a soft pastel scarf around her neck and slipping on her kitten heel sling-backs before she left her room.

On the trip down in the elevator Sara tried to remind herself that she was doing this for Stu and now for Bonny. There was no backing out.

The lift reached the ground floor and Sara walked across the foyer and up a few steps into the raised bar area. She spied Tom at a table but he wasn't alone. Christina, his secretary, was with him. Of course, she suddenly remembered, they had a date.

Sara unexpectedly felt a tug at her heart. It was ridiculous. Why shouldn't Tom move on? The divorce papers were on their way to the lawyer. But even so, seeing Tom with another woman made her feel unreasonably possessive.

Suddenly, as she approached the couple, a little voice inside her head demanded to be heard. *Sara Fielding, this will make it so much easier. He is taken. He's not available so keep your emotions in check.*

Sara watched the way Christina was looking at Tom. Her heart wasn't thrilled at what she saw, but her mind was elated with the couple's body language. They were at ease and relaxed with each other. So relaxed Sara felt sure they must be lovers. She swallowed hard with that thought.

'Tom, Sara's here,' Christina prompted, in little more than a whisper.

Tom turned and his eyes met Sara's. For a split second she felt as if they were the only two people in the room. It wasn't right, she knew it. Perhaps he didn't realise the effect he had on her. But she did and she had to take responsibility for her own thoughts. Right here and right now. She would never step back into Tom's life.

'Sara,' he said, as he stood and pulled out a chair for her. 'I thought you must have fallen asleep, again.'

'I wasn't that long,' she replied brightly, trying to set a light-hearted mood as she sat down. 'In fact, if I wasn't so hungry I'd probably still be in the shower.'

'Speaking of food,' Christina interrupted, 'I'd better be getting home. I want to prepare something special for tomorrow night's dinner with Robert.' She bent down and kissed Tom on the cheek. 'Thanks for the drink and thanks for listening.'

Tom patted her hand. 'Any time.'

'Sorry I can't stop, Sara,' she said, with a smile. 'Perhaps next time we'll be able to chat.'

'That would be nice,' Sara replied, with a curious frown. She watched as Christina slipped her bag over her shoulder and left.

Sara waited until Christina was out of sight before she asked the questions niggling her to distraction.

'Who's Robert? And have I just interrupted your date?'

'Date? With Christina?' he said, glancing over to see his secretary leaving the hotel. 'No, she just wanted to chat about a problem over a drink and get my take on it—some male advice, you could say. But why do you want to know about Robert?'

'No reason,' she lied. 'Just curious.' She hoped Robert was Christina's brother or friend. It meant there was still room for Tom in Christina's life.

'Well, to answer your question, he's her husband. He's been away on business for a fortnight,' Tom replied, quite happy that Sara cared.

Sara's face fell with disappointment. 'So she has a husband yet she needs you to listen to her problems...?'

Tom shot her a wry look. 'She didn't know how to break the news to her husband that she'd written off his uninsured Audi. But, come on, Sara, what's prompted the twenty questions? This isn't like you.'

'Sorry, maybe I'm a bit stressed. I've got a lot on my mind.'

'Then let's talk over dinner. What would you like? Chinese, Italian, seafood?'

What would I like? I'd like Christina to be single. I'd

like you and Christina to be having an affair. And I'd like her to want to marry you and, more importantly, you to want to marry her, giving me some perspective. I'd like to be able to say, and actually believe, that being around you for the next month will be easy. I'd like to rewind to a month ago and leave you outside my hotel room. I'd like my life to be as simple as it has been in Adelaide for the last three years.

'Italian,' Sara replied.

CHAPTER FOUR

THE WOOD OVEN baked pizza was delicious. Sara hadn't realised how hungry she was until she found herself picking up the lonely mushrooms from the empty pizza tray.

'I can order another one,' Tom said drily. 'And then maybe I'll get a look-in.'

Sara wiped the corners of her mouth with the napkin and sat back in the padded booth. She didn't bother answering him. She had seen his hands moving as fast as hers back and forth from the tray.

With a good sleep behind her and now a full stomach, Sara felt ready to sort out the working arrangements so they discussed the rosters, the patient load, the surgical amenities at the hospital and the general planning for the following month.

When they had covered everything, Tom sat back in silence and sipped his drink. His eyes were focused on a spot somewhere in the distance. A place that was taking all his attention.

Slowly he turned his face to hers. 'I know I disappointed you, Sara. As a husband, that is, but I never misled you. I was upfront about the subject of children. I'm sorry that I can't change my mind or give you the all the reasons for my decision. But I've never lied. I just needed to tell you that.'

His sudden statement took her by surprise and added to the emotional see-saw that coming to Melbourne had created.

'I'm sure you had your reasons, just as I have mine. I suppose we should have discussed it all before we married, not after.'

Sara drew breath and with it came a calmer and more resigned disposition. She had to keep emotion out of the equation. She wanted more than Tom would ever be prepared to give. And it had hurt her that he had never been prepared to consider children. She wanted all the joy a family brought, and that money and a career could never replace. The happiness of a child being given a puppy, the first artwork they brought home from school, the cuddle at the end of a day just before they fell asleep. She felt a maternal longing that with each passing year became more difficult to fight.

'I want to hear their laughter, to feel their hugs, to tuck them into bed at night. We're two people with very different priorities. You and your brother have so much in common. You both choose a career over having children. Clearly you have goals you wanted to reach. Becoming associate professor is a huge step and probably not one that would have been easy to achieve with a house full of children. I get it. Really, I do. Your career is your focus and there's no room for anything else.'

'Having a child is not the be-all and end-all…' He faltered, then dropped his gaze without finishing the sentence.

'Not to you, but to me it is,' she said with conviction. 'I couldn't give up on that dream.'

Tom lifted his eyes again to study her face. He had

always wondered what drove this need for children. He understood that the maternal instinct might kick in at a certain age. But it seemed more than this.

Finishing his drink, he decided to ask that very question.

'You know, I really do understand that most women like the idea of having babies and planning big Christmas dinners with the family and all of that,' he said. 'But with you it has always seemed like more. Am I reading too much into it, or am I right in thinking there is something else that drove you to walk away when I wouldn't see it your way?'

Sara wondered why it had taken Tom this long to ask that question. But she sensed it was that he hadn't wanted to know before now. When they had been married and the subject of children had come up, he'd changed it very quickly. Knowing the truth behind her motivations, she suspected, may have put additional pressure on him to consider her reasons and, in turn, her feelings.

'I just love children, I always have and always will,' Sara began slowly. 'And the idea of having to give that up would just mean that history was repeating itself. You already know the number of times in the past that I have had to give in to my parents' wishes. Do what they wanted. Become who they wanted me to be. I do love them, but I had to put my life on hold so many times. It wasn't always obvious, and I'm not sure if was even conscious on their behalf, but I would always end up feeling guilty if I forged ahead without their consent.

'Even as a young child, I frequently had to give up on my own dreams to live theirs. Every time I showed free will, and they thought I might make a decision for myself, they had a way of making me think I was being selfish. But I take responsibility for my feelings. I should have stood up to them and told them I was my own person. It was almost like having my spirit killed with kindness. They were so protective but it was so stifling.'

Tom listened intently. He suddenly felt guilty that he hadn't asked this question before. It had clearly formed a huge part of her childhood.

'So was medicine their dream or yours?'

'No, fortunately my career was a mutual vision. I'm not sure what I would have done if they had wanted me to walk away from that. Perhaps it might have persuaded me to take a stand much earlier.'

'This stand?' Tom cut in, interrupting the story.

'Yes, not to back down and feel guilty about wanting something for myself. I had always done what they expected, I think being an only child made me feel as if I owed them a great debt for bringing me into this world and I had to repay them. To be who they wanted me to be. At least, it always felt that way.'

'I'm sorry to hear that. I had no idea.' Tom looked at his hands absentmindedly and wondered what else he didn't know about his wife.

'In high school I was offered the opportunity to go to Germany for a six-month cultural exchange but my father told me that my mother was about to have more tests and he needed me at home to help take care of her in case the news wasn't good.'

Tom looked surprised to hear this. 'But your mother is fine. Well, she was when we visited her a few years ago. Is she okay now?'

'She's perfectly healthy now but she suffered from benign fibroids and the doctor decided on a myomectomy to remove them. They knew it wasn't a permanent solution in the sense that fibroids can grow back after the procedure. I felt an enormous pressure on me to cancel my trip. I knew they needed me, I couldn't abandon them…could I? The doctor did reassure them both that the condition and surgery wasn't life-threatening but there was more going on than that.

'I remember I wanted to head off with two girlfriends and backpack around Australia and maybe travel over to Italy and Greece after my final year at school. Well, let's just say my friends had a wonderful time but all I saw of the outback and the Mediterranean was on their postcards. My mother's hysterectomy had been scheduled during that time. Apparently my mother was one of the ten per cent that needed a second surgery. The trip had meant so much to me but I felt as if I had to give it up to keep them happy. Honestly, looking back, I don't regret what I gave up, it meant starting my medical study early, but I do wish I had drawn a line in the sand a little earlier.'

'But you all seemed to get on so well whenever I was there.'

'By the time you met them, I'd achieved everything they wanted for me, and during my training I gained back some level of independence. I had proved that I could cope without them and, of course, that they could cope without me. Plus, they loved you, so they were happy with my choice. If they hadn't liked you then I probably would have felt pressured to break up with you.'

'And would you?' he asked, looking intensely into her eyes.

Sara swallowed. 'They loved you, so that question is irrelevant.'

Tom wasn't satisfied. 'That's not an answer to my question, Sara.'

Sara could feel her heart racing. She answered him honestly. 'No, I wouldn't have. I would have told them that being with you was something I wanted more than anything in the world, that it was my dream to spend the rest of my life with you and they would have to live with it.'

Tom felt unashamedly happy with her answer but also immensely guilty. She would have fought for him. He shifted uncomfortably in his seat as he realised what he had done to her. It was her dream to be a mother and she had been fighting him for that right. He had added to the conflicts of her childhood and tried to prevent her right to choose her own path.

'So I was asking the same of you, to give up your dream of children.'

Sara nodded, her heart heavy as she thought back to the sadness of their situation.

'I suppose you thought I would soften to the idea,' he told her. 'Just as I hoped you would move on and be happy with only the two of us.'

'I guess we rushed into our marriage and we paid for the mistake later,' Sara replied.

He sipped his drink and looked thoughtfully at Sara. 'Perhaps we're both still paying.'

The early morning wake-up call had Sara up and about by six. But it wasn't a chore considering how many hours sleep she'd enjoyed. Probably more in the last twenty-four-hour period than in any other since she had chosen a career in oral surgery. And she had needed every minute of it.

Tom had dropped her back at the hotel just before

ten-thirty. They had gone by the practice and he had picked up the notes for the next day's patients. Then, downstairs in a booth near the bar, he had gone over his major surgical list and explained the treatment plans. His work was as accurate and thorough as ever. Sara appreciated the long hours he must have spent to cover the caseload at his practice for both himself and Stu, to oversee the hospital in his new role as associate professor and still have such clear and precise details recorded. She was going to be able to take over without any disruption to the patients at all.

Thankfully there were only consultations and minor surgical cases scheduled for the next two days, so she had time to familiarise herself with everything.

After Tom had left, Sara had reviewed the next day's patients, made her notes and finally given in to sleep at about twelve.

Living in the hotel was not a viable situation. Later in the day she would have to make some calls and arrange a comfortable place that was a little more affordable. She would also have to arrange for someone to pack up the last of her belongings in Adelaide and have them sent on to Texas.

As she pulled underwear from her suitcase and shuffled into the bathroom, her thoughts then wandered to Bonny. She prayed the child's recovery would be easier now her father was with her. She'd often thought that she and Tom would one day have a daughter just like Bonny, and a son…or maybe two of each. Tom was right, she had tried to convince herself that in time he would change his mind about children and realise that they did have the capacity, in terms of time and love, required to raise a family. That their careers were important but the joy they would experience bringing up a child of their own was incomparable.

But you were wrong, Sara admonished herself. He never wanted a child. He reiterated that tonight. So forget the past.

She turned the shower taps on full and enjoyed the very long shower she had wanted the night before as she tried to put outdated dreams from her mind. And know that she was doing what was right for her.

'George Andrews was due at nine. Impressions for his wafer splint. His surgery is in just under two weeks,' Marjorie, the receptionist, informed Sara. 'But his mother just called. They've had car trouble and she's called a taxi. They should be about another fifteen minutes.'

'Thanks,' Sara replied with a smile.

Marjorie was in her early sixties. Her hair was a deep auburn and cut short at the back with flattering soft curls around her forehead. She had a pretty face, with gold rimmed glasses perched on her bob nose. She was about the same height as Sara, just a little bigger in build.

The pair had introduced themselves and as far as Sara could make out, she and Marjorie would get along just fine. The woman did not appear to be the prying type and, with everything on Sara's mind, that was a huge relief.

Sara asked Marjorie not to call her Dr Fielding. Her first name was fine and made her feel more relaxed. But the reason was two-fold. She thought it might also avoid a barrage of questions from patients about her relationship to the other Dr Fielding.

Looking around the rooms, Sara couldn't help but

notice that everything had been completely revamped since she had left three years ago.

She absentmindedly ran her finger over the frame of a painting that hung nearby. A beautiful watercolour of a blue kingfisher. It was new. Everything was new. There was no sign that she had ever been there. It was as if anything she had brought into the practice had disappeared and something else now stood in its place. She wondered if their marital home had been gutted in a similar manner. Had Tom sold her favourite pieces to the highest bidder? She blinked away her unanswered questions and turned her attention back to her surroundings. It was not her business. She had left and Tom did what he wanted. She knew she had no right to judge his actions.

The decor was modern, painted in pastel tones and decorated with light-coloured wooden furniture that had a Scandinavian feel. The spacious waiting room had a large, low pine table covered in magazines, a mix of wooden and chrome chairs lined two walls and there was a wicker basket brimming with toys in the corner of the room. Something to keep little hands amused. Stu's idea, no doubt, Sara surmised. Definitely not Tom's.

Overlooking the waiting room, Marjorie's office was filled with enough computer equipment to run a small NASA project. Sara gently opened the adjoining door to find the fully equipped surgery for minor surgical procedures not needing a general anaesthetic.

She knew that the kitchen and bathroom were located at the back of the rooms. The practice was on the first floor of a quaint old two-storey building that had been totally modernised inside, whilst retaining its exterior character. It was in South Yarra, overlooking the

Yarra River. Sara had always loved the calming effect of the scenery.

Melancholy drew her back to the view and she crossed in earnest to the large picture window. Sara sighed as she took in the vista. The day was cold but the sun was shining down and it was a nice change after the gale the day before. The gentle breeze played with the last of the red-gold leaves of autumn. Weeping branches of the willows dipped in the rippling water near the riverbank. The brown-speckled ducks swam around the row of paddleboats, which were tied together and bobbing with the current at the riverbank.

She closed her eyes for a moment and recalled how a few years ago she and Tom had often stood at the same window. Sometimes they had been so immersed in each other's presence they would barely notice the view. They would hold each other tightly and discuss their days. They understood and respected each other's needs. Two tired bodies moulding as one…

'Penny for your thoughts.'

Sara jumped. She hadn't realised how far her thoughts had travelled until the deep voice broke through.

Tom's voice.

'Um, nothing, nothing at all,' she returned, nervously straightening the lapels of her short navy trench coat and brushing imaginary lint from her matching skirt. 'So, what brings you here? Don't you have a hospital to take care of?'

'Board meeting. I hate those damned things. It's always the same old bickering about increased funding cuts, meaning fewer beds and fewer staff. So I sent Johnson to take notes. That should be eye-opening for everyone, Johnson *and* the board members.' He smiled.

Sara smiled back at him in silence then he noticed the softness suddenly turn to something more professional and reserved as she adjusted her jacket and moved away to the other side of the room.

Tom looked at her, wishing things had been different. Wishing he was able to give her what she wanted and what she deserved in life. She wasn't asking for the world and to any other man it would seem fair and natural to want children. But Tom couldn't provide that. Fatherhood would never be a part of his life. He could accept it but it wouldn't be fair to keep Sara in his self-imposed childless life so he had to keep his distance.

Stirring up old feelings again would only delay the inevitable. Even if they rekindled their love, she would leave and turn his life upside down all over again for the very same reason.

Marjorie walked in from the kitchen. 'I've put the kettle on. Will you both have a cup of tea or coffee?'

'Yes, that would be lovely,' Sara answered hurriedly.

'Not for me,' Tom replied. 'I was just leaving. I'm needed back at the hospital—it was just a quick visit.' His sentence was cut short when the door opened. Tom took this cue and left. It had been a short visit, with no purpose other than to spend a few minutes with Sara. He knew he couldn't change their fate. The divorce would seal that but he had a month to enjoy her company, as a doctor he admired and a woman he desired. He was torturing himself just being near her, but he was unable to stop.

Sara watched him leave then turned her attention to a boy in his late teens and the older woman who had entered the office.

'George, Mrs Andrews,' Marjorie greeted them

cheerily. 'Please, take a seat. Dr Fielding, I mean Sara, will be right with you.'

'Where's Dr Anderson?' George asked anxiously. The metal braces on his teeth caught the light. 'Isn't he seeing me today?'

Sara stepped forward. 'No, George. Dr Anderson won't be seeing you today,' she began. 'He had to spend some time with his family. His little girl isn't very well and he asked me to step in and look after you and all of his patients. I'll be carrying out your operation.'

George had looked a little anxious when he walked in but now his worries seemed to escalate to distress. Surgery for anyone was a stressful time but Sara was aware that for an adolescent it was doubly so.

'Don't worry, George,' Sara told him. 'I won't do anything without first explaining it to you and if you have any questions, please, ask me. In a moment we'll go and take some moulds of your teeth, which will be sent off to a lab. The technician will use these moulds to make a special splint, called a wafer, and I will use this to position your jaws during surgery. I'm sure you've had impressions before.'

The boy nodded but his expression was guarded.

'I know they're a bit mucky but they don't hurt. Your orthodontist has put special pins in your braces in preparation for this. We call them high hats, and they make it easier for me to do my job.'

'Yeah, and they stick out a bit,' George complained, and pulled his lips down over the braces.

'How long will it take today?' Mrs Andrews cut in.

'Not very long at all,' Sara replied, turning her attention to the woman. 'You're most welcome to come in.'

'I'm not a child, Mum,' George growled. 'Just wait out here.'

Mrs Andrews raised her eyebrows and sat down. She clearly knew it was pointless to argue with a teenager. Sara smiled to herself. She doubted that George's bravado would hold up just prior to surgery. Then without doubt he would want his mother close by.

'Well, let's go and get started,' Sara said, and led George off towards the consulting room. Marjorie followed closely behind, leaving Mrs Andrews sifting through the magazines. The appointment didn't take much longer than twenty minutes. George didn't ask too many questions but with a mouthful of impression material that would have been difficult. After the impressions were checked by Sara, then packed and taken to Reception to be collected by the laboratory courier, Sara asked Mrs Andrews to come in.

Sara clipped the X-rays onto the wall viewer and studied them for a moment. 'Are there any questions?'

'Are there lots of guys with this problem?' George asked, rubbing his very pronounced lower jaw.

'Guys and girls,' Sara reassured him. 'You have what we call a skeletal class-three malocclusion. This means that your lower jaw is forward in relation to your upper jaw. I'm sure Dr Anderson has gone over this with you but it happened because your mandible, or lower jaw, has grown more than your upper. It's a case of one didn't grow enough and the other grew too much.'

'So you're going to pull my jaw back?'

'Not exactly.' Sara looked at the X-ray viewer, where a profile of George's skull was illuminated. 'You have a skeletal discrepancy. So Dr Anderson had planned on surgery to advance the upper jaw.' Sara pointed to the relevant facial features on the X-ray as she spoke. She moved the tiny mouth ruler she used as a pointer down to the lower jaw area as she continued. 'And set back the lower jaw. Just think of your lower jaw coming back and your upper jaw moving forward about the same amount until they sort of meet halfway and then surgery on your chin to make it a little less angular or severe.'

'I think I kind of get it,' George said. 'But I told Dr Anderson that I didn't like my nose much and he said he could fix that too.'

Sara thought it best to keep clear of decisions that were purely cosmetic. 'George, I think it's best if you and the family make that decision at home. Just call Marjorie next week if you want me to proceed with a rhinoplasty at the same time—that's the name we give to the nose operation.'

'But what do you think?' George asked, giving unexpected value to Sara's opinion on the matter.

Sara was flattered that he had asked her but she had to remain impartial. 'To be honest, George, it is a cosmetic improvement and therefore has to be a family decision. No surgeon can tell you what you should or shouldn't look like when it comes to nose shape or chin shape.'

'But if he was your son, what would you advise us to do?' George's mother asked.

Sara was taken aback by the question. *If he was my son?* She stared down at her hands clasped tightly in her lap. If I ever have a son, she thought, I would want only the best for him. I would want him to grow into a strong, perceptive individual just like Tom. Her stomach tightened a little at her reaction. Day one and Tom Fielding had safely tucked himself into her subconscious. Just where she didn't need him.

She swallowed as she looked at Mrs Andrews and George, then thoughtfully she answered, 'I wouldn't rush into any surgery on a whim. I would think it through, discuss it at home and be very sure it was something George felt very strongly about undertaking.'

She blinked away her other thoughts. It was going to be long month in Melbourne.

Sara switched off the X-ray viewer, slipped the X-rays inside the case notes and then escorted the young man and his mother back into the waiting room.

'Sara, your nine-thirty appointment, Mollie Hatcher, is here,' Marjorie said as the three approached the front desk.

Sara remembered reading Mollie's referral notes and when the child smiled nervously, Sara could see the large fleshy membrane that ran between her front teeth, giving her a gap large enough to hold a gold coin. The referring doctor had recommended a frenectomy to remove it, and even before the consultation, Sara had judged that to be the right treatment plan.

Looking over the medical history, Sara ushered in the little girl and her mother.

It was another half hour consultation, which ended with Mrs Hatcher booking a time for Mollie's minor surgery in the rooms the following week.

The day continued, with Sara seeing a steady load of Stu's patients. Most of them were new patient referrals and there were three post-operative check-ups. Tom had stepped in to cover Stu's consulting role at the hospital and Sara would be picking up Tom's private patients. It was a sensible arrangement for the weeks ahead.

She knew the next day it would be Tom's patients and a minor surgical list in the afternoon. Both men were professional and skilled surgeons and Sara hadn't disagreed with any treatment plan either had suggested for their patients. She knew the next day would be no exception. When it came to work, that was the one area that she and Tom would never come to loggerheads. He had taught her well and she would never doubt his decision. His knowledge as a consultant and his dexterity as a surgeon were second to none.

Sara was quietly honoured he had approved her stepping into the practice that he had built over many years and had then invited Stu to join. And she was pleased to be doing it without any intervention from him. He did trust her. From someone with a reputation of being one of the finest surgeons in the country, that was a huge accolade for her.

It was about six o'clock when Sara realised she had done nothing about accommodation. She would have to spend another night at the hotel and then tomorrow she had to organise something else.

Marjorie said goodnight, locked up and left for the day. Sara was tidying up the last of the case notes when she heard a key in the front door. It didn't take her long to realise who it was.

'I'm in the office, Tom. Just a few bits and pieces to tidy up.'

She heard his footsteps draw nearer and looked up to find him framed in the doorway. His face was a little drawn but still unbelievably handsome. His jaw was darkened by the first signs of fine stubble.

'I'm here to take you home.'

'That's very sweet of you,' Sara remarked. 'But I've already booked a taxi to my hotel.'

Tom crossed the room in silence. His dark eyes didn't stray from her face for a moment. 'I wasn't talking about the hotel, Sara. I'm taking you to our home.'

CHAPTER FIVE

SARA WAS STUNNED into silence.

She swallowed a lump of emotions that had converged in her throat. *Our home.* There was no 'our' anything any more. She chewed nervously on the inside of her cheek. What on earth was Tom thinking? She felt herself falling into the deep, grey eyes that were focused solely upon her. She wanted to pull away, she had to, but she couldn't pull away far enough. Her gaze dropped only to his wide, soft mouth.

A mouth that her heart could suddenly remember giving her the most tender of kisses. Sara felt so confused. Confused about her own feelings. Even more confused about Tom's. She thought they had set the parameters. She was not about to move back in with him on either a short-term or long-term basis.

Did he think by her staying in Melbourne that she would throw away her new life and come back to him? He must know after their talk the night before that she wouldn't back down. She wanted children, and it was not negotiable. Then was he looking for another few nights of passion for old times' sake? She couldn't, and she wouldn't allow him to change her plans. Her mind had to take over. Calculated logic had to kick in. She had to control her body's desire for him. If she didn't,

Sara was terrified of where it all might lead. Heartbreak, no doubt, for both of them.

'There is no *our* any more, Tom.'

'You can call it my house if it makes you feel any better.'

'It does,' she returned. 'Because it's the truth. I don't belong in Melbourne. I don't have any ties here any more.' Sara closed the file of paperwork she was completing.

'I'm just trying to help,' he argued. 'Unless, of course, you'd rather pay for accommodation at the hotel for the next month.'

'So moving in with you is the best solution? I hardly think so.'

'Not with me exactly. The other half of the maisonette, the part that belonged to Mrs Vandercroft, is now mine. She moved into a nursing home only a month after you...' Tom hesitated, not wanting to make her feel that he was blaming her for their separation.

'Well, just after we parted, so I bought it. You remember how she had one or two falls, well, they increased and finally she really injured herself on a coffee table she just didn't see. Her eyesight was failing, and she was unsteady on her feet. Her family didn't want her living alone any more and, as you know, they all lived interstate. Anyway, she had just turned ninety-eight and didn't want to haul herself up to Sydney so she moved into a nursing home not too far away. I just use the place for storage, so you can have it for the month. I was going to offer it to the locum anyway. I had no idea it would be you.'

Sara considered him suspiciously then felt a little silly for overreacting. Perhaps it was an offer with no strings. After all, he had signed the divorce papers. And he had an empty place.

She shook herself mentally. He definitely appeared to have his emotions in check.

'Well, does this silence mean you're considering my offer?' he asked, jolting her out of her thoughts.

Sara closed her eyes for a split second. She had no logical argument for refusing his offer. Only her irrational thoughts. Against her better judgement she made a decision and prayed for everyone's sake that she was doing the right thing.

'I suppose it's a sensible idea.'

But even as the words passed over her lips, weighty doubts rang alarm bells loudly in her mind. But that was her problem, not his.

Tom smiled. He knew their time together would be short-lived but apart from the great love life they had shared, he enjoyed spending time with Sara. He always had. She challenged him. She was his equal on so many levels. He just wanted a few more weeks with her and then he knew he would let her go. Let her start her new life and not make her think twice about her decision. He hoped this time when she left it might be easier. He hoped his heart wouldn't shatter this time.

As they pulled into the driveway Sara felt a tightening in her chest. They had collected her things from the hotel and made their way to his home about twenty minutes from the city. It was a corner property in a suburb filled with double-fronted cottages and bungalows.

Lit by the headlights of the car, the house looked the same as it did the day she had left. It had been one of the hardest days of her life. She had walked away from her home and her marriage, even though she had still been very much in love with her husband.

The cream stucco walls and shiny gunmetal-grey roof with green gutters hadn't changed. She and Tom had planned to have the front facade steamed-cleaned to reveal the bluestone lying beneath the thick paint but their schedules had never given them the time. It had been something they'd always put off, thinking they had plenty of time in the future.

The roses were in bloom, the way they had been that day in June three years ago. Huge open cabbage roses in deep reds and pastel pinks lined the gravel path to the front door.

Tears welled in the back of her eyes and threatened to spill over.

'Let me get that,' Tom said, as Sara reached into the boot of his late-model Lexus. Their hands touched as they tried to retrieve her luggage. His soft skin brushed against hers. Sara released her hold on the bag immediately and turned away. His touch was unsettling.

'I've got a key for you somewhere in my pocket,' he told her, as he closed the boot and followed behind her, his footsteps crunching on the gravel all the way up to the front door.

Sara's mind was anywhere but in the present and she struggled to keep on track.

'Here it is.' He handed her a key chained to a small crystal slipper. It was the one she had bought when they'd first moved into the house. She couldn't believe he had kept it all this time.

'You know, I always thought this was a little kitsch considering your good taste.'

She held the keyring in her open palm and stared at it in silence.

She remembered back to the day she had bought it. It had been the day before they'd left Prague, where they had spent three days of their four-week honeymoon. Strolling along a cobbled street, they had stumbled upon a little shop that was filled with the most beautiful crystal. Sara had spied the slipper and had known she had to have it. Tom had wanted to buy a beautifully cut crystal vase but she bought the slipper, never telling him the reason.

It was because their romance had been like a fairytale. Having the crystal keyring ensured she was never going to lose her keys, or her Prince Charming. But she knew better than to tell Tom. The logical man that he was, he never would have understood. His diagnosis would have been to tell her she was completely crazy.

Of course, he could have no idea what she was going through now. The memories, the guilt of leaving, it all came flooding back and she wanted so desperately to fall into his arms and pretend that the three years they spent apart were all a bad dream. But she couldn't. Standing there together, she knew she still did have strong feelings for him but that they weren't enough to build a life upon. She wanted more and she knew she had every right to ask for more.

'It's getting mighty cold, standing here while you admire the keyring, Sara.'

Sara looked up and him and wished she could brush aside her feelings and offer a witty retort, but she couldn't. She had agreed in the car on the way home that they would eat their takeaway dinner together, but suddenly she felt too fragile to honour her promise. The house, the keyring, they had brought too many memories to the surface and she needed time alone to sort through these feelings and put them away. Time without Tom.

'I'm sorry,' she began, rubbing her temples in a circular motion, 'but I have this splitting headache. Would you mind terribly if we didn't have dinner together? I wouldn't be very good company.'

Tom considered her for a moment in the soft light from the streetlamp. She felt that his silence hinted at disbelief but he didn't confirm it with his words.

'Of course not,' he finally uttered, and handed her the box with her dinner inside.

Sara graciously took the warm package and unlocked the front door then felt along the wall for the light switch.

'I'll call over if I need anything,' she called back, before wheeling her luggage inside and closing the door on the cold night air. And on Tom. She just wished her heart could do the same.

The maisonette was the reverse floor plan of the one that she and Tom had shared next door. Dropping her case to the floor, Sara's steps echoed down the polished hallway as she made her way into the sitting room.

The maisonette was furnished nicely but it was the antithesis of the home they had shared. It lacked the character of the home they had decorated together. With modern furniture not unlike that in the waiting room at the practice, she would be comfortable and it would be more than adequate for the month.

Tom closed the door to his maisonette, wondering what Sara was doing. Was she eating, unpacking or had she collapsed from the first day on the job? She was actually staying in his side of the maisonette. He had been living there for the last three years as he couldn't live amongst the memories of the furniture that surrounded him tonight.

This was actually the house he had intended to offer

the locum but he couldn't let Sara stay there. It was still furnished with all their belongings. For the next four weeks he would be staying in the home he used for storage. He couldn't let her know that he had kept everything. He didn't want her to know that he hadn't been able to give it away but he also couldn't live amongst it. Not yet. She had moved on…he hadn't.

He loved everything they had bought together but that was the problem—they had bought it together. When they had been happy and in love and planning their future. Tom had called his cleaning lady to move his clothes and toiletries and books from one side to the other when he'd found out Sara was working for the month.

He went to the kitchen to find a fork and then ate his dinner on his lap. He could hear Sara moving about and unpacking through the thin walls.

Even though it would only be for a few short weeks it felt like she was home. But he knew neither of them had the power to do the slightest thing about changing the paths that would eventually lead them away from one another for ever.

Half an hour later Sara threw the remains of her dinner in the bin. She was hungry and she had picked at the pasta but her churning stomach hadn't allowed her to finish it.

She worried about how she would deal with the proximity of Tom. She still loved him. She wondered if he knew it too.

'Damn you,' she cursed under her breath.

Why couldn't he talk about their differences? Tell her the reason he didn't want children in his life? Was he really that selfish or was there something that made him hate the thought of children? She had tried so hard to understand when they had been married but he'd shut the conversation down every time she'd brought it up.

She knew his brother, Heath an ENT specialist, hadn't had any children either. Sara hadn't spent much time with him as he had lived in Los Angeles with his wife until they'd divorced. It hadn't appeared to be an unhappy marriage but, like Sara, his wife had wanted children. Sara wasn't sure if that had been the precursor to her leaving or not. Shortly after the split, Heath had moved to San Francisco to practise. Although she'd seen him with Tom both times he had visited Melbourne, the subject of children had never been discussed. It was like both brothers had decided not to have children and that was final. It was a taboo subject. The elephant in the room.

Was there something in their past that stopped them from wanting a family? Sara doubted that. Whenever Tom had spoken of his parents, both of whom had passed away before Tom and Sara had begun dating, the memories he'd relayed of his childhood had been happy. He and his brother had shared a love of BMX bikes as teenagers and had then dropped that sport to both study medicine. It appeared a happy upbringing.

Sara had wanted more than a blanket refusal to discuss the idea of children. She wanted to know the truth but instead came up against his stubborn refusal to talk. She was forced to accept that his stubbornness went hand in hand with selfishness. She still wondered if there was more to it.

Despite how difficult it was to fight her feelings, Sara knew nothing could happen between them. Tom's timing was all wrong. She was leaving to start a new life.

Don't ruin it, Sara, don't put your life back on hold,

she told herself as she finished unpacking. She knew it would lead to resentment, that she would be sacrificing what she wanted and needed to keep him happy.

It won't work with Tom and you know it, she told herself. Then why did she have to feel so at home? A feeling she hadn't experienced since she had left the same house three years ago. A sense of belonging.

She put a little hot water in the sink and washed her cutlery and glass. As she dried and put them away in the drawer she decided to take a nice long soak in a bath.

There was no point in analysing her curious feelings towards Tom, she decided as she slipped into the steamy bubbles and tried to soak away her troubles. It was just reverie and lost love playing games with her emotions. It was over and they both knew it. It was an *itch*, that was all. Some time later, after almost drifting off to sleep, she stepped from the deep tub, towel-dried her warm body and slipped into her pyjamas and dressing gown.

It wouldn't take long to regain control of her feelings, she resolved. She lay back on the sofa and pulled a patterned rug over herself. It was so cold. She looked over at the heater. It was the same old gas style they had next door. And she knew she could never light it. She didn't want to call Tom and ask for his assistance but she also didn't want to wake up with chilblains in her toes.

'It's just me.'

'Hi, me.'

Sara wished for a moment that she hadn't called. Running her fingers through her short, damp hair, she worried about depending upon him for anything. She pulled the rug and her knees up under her chin, perhaps it wasn't *that* cold. She'd felt unexpectedly awkward talking to him on the phone, knowing he was next door. It was odd. She felt so at home, knowing Tom was only the other side of the wall.

Finally, she mustered her thoughts and asked him to come over and help her light the heater. It sounded like a call to a repairman. Businesslike and distant.

Her fingers and toes were quickly becoming icicles, but two minutes later she heard Tom's speedy knock.

'Hello, Sara,' he muttered, as she opened the door. He smiled wryly. 'How's the headache?'

Sara frowned at the question. The way he looked made her fumble over her words and forget momentarily that she had used the headache as an excuse to get away from him. He was standing on her porch in a dark blue dressing gown. It wrapped over low down and exposed his bare, toned chest. His hair was dishevelled and his face was shadowed with fine stubble. His legs were naked and his feet were inside leather slippers.

'Hello...Tom,' she replied, dragging her eyes back to his. She was so angry with herself. It wasn't as if she hadn't been around good-looking men over the years. In fact, she'd dated one or two handsome men. But her reaction was more than that. She suspected that it was being aware, very aware of what lay beneath Tom's loosened robe that made her feel this way.

He began shivering, pulled his robe tighter and started to rub his arms vigorously. 'Could I come inside and light the gas heater before they have to cart me away suffering from frostbite to the extremities?'

Sara nodded. 'Oh, God, I'm sorry,' she said, and stepped away from the door, allowing Tom to move past her.

'So you're feeling okay, then?'

She closed the door on the frozen night air. 'I'm fine,

truly...actually, I haven't felt better. The headache's gone. I just needed to soak in a tub for...' She paused and glanced nervously down at her watch. 'Gosh, absolutely ages. But I'm glad I did. I'll need a clear head tomorrow, I've got a full day with minor surgery. Two sets of wisdom teeth to be removed, an exposure of a canine and a few others that I can't recall off the top of my head.' She felt her heart racing and couldn't believe how she had prattled on like a nervous teenager. Why did he do this to her? It wasn't fair. She just wanted him to light the fire and leave.

Tom's mouth curved to a smile. 'They're all my patients. So make sure you do a good job, won't you?'

Sara was grateful that he had chosen to ignore her ramblings and she took his sarcastic cue. 'I'll try really hard not to lose any of them for you,' she returned drily.

He walked over to the heater, catching some creaking floorboards on the way. Standing with his back to her, he reached for the box of matches on the mantelpiece. He squatted on the ground and lit the heater. It was old but Sara remembered how quickly it heated the room. She blinked and looked away before she had time to admire his broad-shouldered physique for too long.

'Thank you, Tom,' she said, as she walked over to warm her hands by the heater. 'I'm sorry that you had to come over to do that. I never did get the hang of lighting the old heater.'

'Just what a good landlord does.'

'Of course, I forgot to ask how much you would like in rent for the place while I'm here.'

Tom looked at Sara in silence. She was trying to turn every part of their lives into a business arrangement. He knew why. And he understood she would be leaving when Stu returned. He wouldn't fight it. But he was glad to have her living close. It was almost like old times. She was all rugged up in flannelette pyjamas and fluffy slippers, her face scrubbed bare of make-up, and she was still the most desirable woman in the world.

'What figure are you looking at?' she asked. 'Three hundred, three fifty?'

Money was the furthest thing from his mind. She was a part of the house and his heart and if she had nowhere else she needed to be, she could stay for ever.

'I'm happy to pay four hundred, if that's closer to the mark...'

'Sara, I don't want anything for the place. You are doing me a favour, filling in for Stu...'

'And you are reimbursing me well,' she cut in.

'I know but that's immaterial. You can have the place...for a coffee. I need to stay awake to go over some reports so I could do with a short—'

'Short black, no sugar,' she finished his order. She smiled. It was so easy. It was like the three years had never passed. Here they were together in the house, in their pyjamas. She hated the fact that she wanted so badly to reach out and feel his arms around her. To cuddle up in front of the fire with the sound of the rain on the metal roof. To hold each other till they fell asleep, just like they'd used to.

She snapped out of it and headed for the kitchen and turned on the coffee machine. She looked back at Tom, standing by the fire. Looking so good. It wasn't fair. He was almost the perfect man. And he *was* the perfect lover.

CHAPTER SIX

MORNING CAME QUICKLY AGAIN. Sara thought she might find it difficult to sleep with Tom only on the other side of the wall but she'd fallen into a deep and restful sleep quickly. Almost the moment her head had hit the pillow.

Climbing out of bed, she showered, applied light make-up and dressed in camel-coloured trousers and a striped black and camel fine-knit sweater. She intended to throw her overcoat on top before she left. The number to call for a cab to the practice was already on her phone. Unexpectedly, there was a knock at the door.

As she opened the door, she saw Tom, dressed in dark woollen slacks, a black sweater and heavy grey overcoat, his keys in his hand.

'I trust you slept well.'

'Very,' she told him, as she took a step backwards and held the door open for him to come inside.

Tom walked in, swinging the keys around his finger playfully.

'Do you intend telling me what the keys are for?' she asked.

'Mrs Vanderbilt sold me the house and her car. At ninety-eight, she thought it was better to get off the road. I didn't argue with her—in fact, I told her it was a wise decision considering all the idiots out there now.

And that's how I came to be the owner of the 1967 Austin Healey in your driveway.'

Sara forgot about everything as she crossed the room excitedly. She knelt on the armchair and pulled back the lace drapes. With her sweater sleeve she wiped a small circle of fog from the window. There in the driveway was a mint-green Austin Healey, its duco and chrome shining in the dappled morning sun. She hadn't seen it the night before as it had been too dark when they'd arrived home. Sara adored old cars, old houses and old furniture. They had so much character and history to offer.

She turned around and beamed. 'Tom, it's so sweet of you to let me drive it. I swear I'll be so careful.'

'You can't be serious,' he said with a smirk, as he threw the keys across the room to her. 'You can drive my Lexus. I'm the only one who drives the Healey!'

A little after eight o'clock Sara pulled into the car park of the surgery in Tom's late-model Lexus. She'd had a light breakfast of cereal and toast from the contents of the fridge and pantry that she assumed Tom had stocked for her. Marjorie had just arrived and they walked into the building together.

'Not that it's any of my business, Sara, but tell me, did you decide to move in to Tom's house?'

Sara didn't try to hide her surprise. 'How on earth did you know about that?'

'Then you did?' Marjorie smiled broadly as she slipped her car keys inside her bag and patted it closed. 'Very sensible idea, Sara, very sensible. I think everything will work out quite nicely.'

Sara wasn't too sure if she should read anything in to Marjorie's comments but decided to let it go.

'It will save me a considerable amount of money over the month.'

'Lisa, his cleaning lady, dusted and polished everything, moved his things and stocked the fridge and pantry for you. Tom certainly makes our lives hectic, but we manage.'

'Moved *his* things?'

Marjorie realised that she had said too much. 'Just some boxes and bits and bobs he stored there.'

The cover-up worked and Sara didn't bother asking the woman any more questions. She picked up her pace and headed towards the door.

'I bet you were busy,' Sara said. 'Almost as busy as we'll be today.' She changed the subject as they rode up in the lift. To move further from the subject of Tom and her living arrangements, Sara asked about the fantastic network of linked computers that occupied most of the front office. Thankfully, Marjorie obliged with a lengthy discussion about her big toys and dropped the subject of her employer.

Sara had consultations with new patients all morning and was looking forward to the afternoon surgery. Being so busy kept her mind on track and most importantly off Tom.

She and Marjorie both chose something nice and light from the assorted sandwiches that the lunch delivery girl brought around. The anaesthetist, William North, arrived about one o'clock and so did the part-time nurse, Laura, whom Tom and Stu employed for the days of surgical procedures. After introductions and a friendly chat they were ready to begin the afternoon list.

'Melanie Sanders,' Marjorie called softly across the waiting room. 'The doctors are ready now if you would like to follow me.'

Melanie was seventeen years old and needed her impacted wisdom teeth removed. She had been sitting nervously with her mother.

'Hi, Melanie, I'm Sara and I'm filling in for Dr Fielding for a few weeks while he is at the hospital. So if it's all right with you, let's get started and remove those teeth that have been giving you trouble.'

While Melanie climbed into the operating chair, Sara scrubbed in, slipped on her latex gloves and a pale yellow disposable gown.

'Melanie, Dr North will give you a little shot in the hand, which will make you feel a bit drowsy. You will still be awake and able to follow instructions but you won't feel any pain, and as a bonus the amnesiac properties of the anaesthetic means you won't remember anything about this operation when you get home.'

Laura pinned a surgical bib around Melanie and then William began the sedation. It quickly took effect and Sara was able to begin the removal of the offending teeth. The X-rays were illuminated on the wall beside the chair. The procedure went well and forty-five minutes, and numerous sutures later, the four teeth had been removed and Laura escorted the patient to the recovery room.

William and Sara scrubbed and prepared for the next patient while Marjorie prepared the small surgery again.

The next patient was booked in for a similar removal of wisdom teeth. Luckily, this one was straightforward and he was soon in the recovery room.

Sara and William took a short break and were about to prepare for their third patient when Marjorie asked her to take a telephone call. It was George Andrews' mother. And it was urgent.

'It's Sara Fielding, Mrs Andrews. How can I help?'

'Sara, it's about George, he's refusing to have the operation. The other boys he mixes with have filled his head with worries. He's convinced he could die on the operating table or end up with brain damage or a jaw that has no feeling.'

Sara rubbed her forehead with the inside of her wrist. It wasn't the first time she had encountered friends throwing in their unwanted advice and worrying a patient unnecessarily.

'Don't worry, Mrs Andrews. I'm more than happy to talk to George. I'm sure between the two of us we can convince him he needs to finish his orthodontic treatment and have the operation.'

'I'm not so sure but, Sara, if he doesn't have the surgery now, I know he'll never do it. His friends have persuaded him to move up north and work as a jackaroo.'

'You leave it to me, Mrs Andrews. But it's important for George to undergo the surgery because he wants to. He'll be an adult in a few months and he should be making his own decisions. Even so, they should be informed decisions not something based on the imaginary fears of his friends.'

'I hope you can convince him because, goodness knows, we've tried everything,' Mrs Andrews confided.

Sara flipped open the appointment book. Her eyes scanned over the pages. There wasn't a time free during surgery hours for nearly three weeks and that would be too late. She would have to stay late one evening.

'Friday at seven,' Sara told her. 'Can you both be here then?'

'I'll do my best.'

Sara hung up the telephone. At that moment she wished she had the counselling skills of Tom. She knew that she was more than competent, but Tom seemed to have the edge when it came to handling patient anxieties.

With a sigh, Sara pursed her lips and returned to the surgery, where she scrubbed and prepared for the next patient. She studied the X-rays while Laura popped the young girl in the reclining chair. The patient's canine tooth had developed in the palate, so it needed to be exposed and brought into position.

'I'm Sara and I will be doing your minor operation today. Has Dr Fielding explained it to you?'

The young girl nodded and opened her mouth. She clearly wanted to get it over and done with. Sara explained what the anaesthetist would be doing and then they were ready to begin.

William started sedation while Sara checked the trays had everything ready for both the surgical procedure and then the bonding of the attachment. When she was quite sure that Josie would be free of pain, she began the procedure of exposing the tooth. Laura was an experienced nurse in oral surgery procedures and assisted Sara to attach the bracket to the exposed tooth. A fine surgical chain was attached to the bracket before being linked to the metal braces.

The bracket held well and Sara was happy that the tooth should move down into position over a few months. It wasn't long before the patient was resting comfortably in Recovery.

There were four more patients on the afternoon list and it had just passed six o'clock when the final patient left for home. Sara had enjoyed working with William and Laura and thanked them for their work.

'Any time,' William said.

'Ditto,' agreed Laura, and they both headed off.

Closing the door on the pair, Sara remembered she still had to make some calls about George Andrews.

'Marjorie,' she called aloud, trying to determine her location in the rooms.

'I'm tidying up the recovery room, Sara.'

Sara walked quickly in her direction, talking as she went.

'Do you recall any young male adolescent, class-three malocclusions who underwent surgical correction around twelve months ago?' Sara entered the small room as she finished her question.

After fluffing up the last of the generously proportioned cushions that rested on the sofa in the recovery room, Marjorie stood upright. She tilted her head to one side, thinking.

'I'd have to check. Why do you ask?'

'The phone call from Mrs Andrews. Her son George now has reservations about the surgery and I thought if he could have a word with boys around his own age who had undergone the operation, then he might feel better about it.'

'Seems like a swimming idea to me. Are you going to check with Tom before you contact them?'

'No,' Sara told her bluntly. 'I am here in place of Dr Anderson. So any decision I choose to make does not have to be seconded by Dr Fielding. He's far too busy at the hospital to ask for his opinion on something like this.'

'Whatever you think is best,' Marjorie remarked as she slipped past and made her way into the office.

Sara didn't reply. She knew it had come out a little too assertively but she needed to let Marjorie know that she was running the practice. And she needed to keep Tom as far away as humanly possible. To ensure their contact was limited to the absolute minimum. She had hoped it would be easier by now. But it wasn't. And now she doubted it ever would be.

She followed in silence and waited for Marjorie to produce the patient's records.

'I do know what you to are up to,' Marjorie said matter-of-factly.

Sara stopped in her tracks. 'I'm sorry, what did you just say?'

'That you are trying to be all independent and keep Dr Fielding at bay. But if you need to keep him at bay, that says enough for me.'

'Not dragging Dr Fielding back here doesn't explain anything other than the need to allow him to stay focused on his busy schedule at the hospital. He is associate professor after all.'

'I know how important Tom is to the hospital, Sara, but I think he's also very important to you. Perhaps you don't like being too close because you still have feelings for him,' she said, as she sat down in front of her office desk. 'Take some advice from me and don't leave it too late.'

'Too late for what?'

'To start living life again,' Marjorie began, swivelling on her chair to face Sara. 'I know for a fact that Tom hasn't been. He's been cooped up here or, according to Christina, making up any excuse to stay late at the hospital. He has no sign of a social or romantic life. It's just such a waste when a young person forgets to actually enjoy life.'

Sara was stunned. Perhaps it was his workload and, of course, the PhD would have consumed his time along, with maintaining the practice and keeping up his hours at the hospital. He had probably been doing fourteen-hour days.

She didn't want to believe that perhaps he was still hurting over the separation. Because if that was the case, surely he would have contacted her during the last three years? Reached out and said he wanted to discuss the unresolved issues in their marriage? But he hadn't. He was a stubborn man who would not change his mind and negotiate. Neither could she on something so important. Her days of backing down, of putting her needs last were over.

'Tom's social life has nothing to do with me, Marjorie. Now, if I could have those records, please. I have some calls to make.'

Marjorie's smile didn't mask her doubt at Sara's remarks as she handed over the patient's charts in silence. But something about Marjorie's disposition made Sara realise that the subject was not finished, at least not in the other woman's eyes. But a busybody receptionist was still the least of Sara's concerns.

It was around seven by the time Sara had spoken to both the boys and their families and explained the reason for her call. Thankfully they both agreed and Sara set a date for them to come in near the end of the week. She then called George's home and confirmed with his mother that he would attend one last consultation.

In allowing the boys to speak with George and for him to see their successful surgical outcomes, Sara hoped it would convince him that the results of the operation outweighed the risks.

After locking up the practice, Sara headed off to pick up dinner from a Mexican takeaway she had spied on the way to work. She vowed to get out to the supermarket the next day. The front porch light was on when Sara pulled into the driveway. It was a welcoming sight. But she could never admit it. Not to Tom. Not really even to herself.

With her takeaway in one hand and her briefcase in the other, Sara made her way up the gravel path. It was cold outside and the warm breath of her yawn made a fine steam in the crisp night air.

'Hello, there, Doc. Need some help?' Tom's familiar voice came closer with each word until he was upon her.

'No I'm fine, really I—' she started to say, before she felt him tugging at her briefcase. She struggled to retain ownership and suddenly a warm hand encircled her wrist. It was a powerful grip but tender enough to not bruise her skin. She froze. She didn't want to have these confusing feelings. His touch was unsettling. It was like a burning torch on her skin that spread a dangerous heat through her body. As much as Sara valued her imported leather briefcase, she didn't want to feel any part of Tom's body touching hers.

Her fingers purposely slipped from the handle. The briefcase fell heavily to the ground with a thud and then a crunch as it skidded across the loose gravel. Sara cringed as she imagined the scratches and tears across the fine surface but it was worth the toll to feel his hand finally release its hold on her wrist.

'What just happened?' he asked sharply. 'Do you dislike me touching you that much, Sara?'

No. I like it too much, she thought. Time had not dimmed her body's response to him and that was what she hated.

'It's nothing to do with you,' she lied. 'I'm tired and I want to eat this…' she held up the paper bag '…before it goes cold and soggy.'

'Well, why not just say so?' he demanded.

'You'd manacled me like a prisoner. You didn't give me much choice.' It wasn't true but she couldn't help her reaction.

Tom didn't reply. He just shook his head and walked away in silence. Sara wanted to run after him and apologise. She had overreacted and her behaviour had been rude. She realised what she'd done and what she'd said had been wrong. Tom certainly couldn't be held responsible for how her heart was feeling. Or for the desire he was stirring in her soul. But apologising would only bring him back and she needed to keep her distance. She needed time to sort out her feelings. Sara pulled up the collar of her coat against the cold breeze as Tom slammed his front door shut.

Sara realised she would have to work harder at controlling her feelings if she was going to get through the next month. Without doubt it was going to be the longest four weeks of her life.

CHAPTER SEVEN

MARJORIE HANDED SARA the mail. 'There's one addressed to you and it's from the country,' she said in an enthusiastic tone.

Sara was surprised. All of the correspondence that she had been dealing with was addressed to either Tom or Stu and all related to patient referrals or reports. But this large envelope was addressed to her.

Curiosity made her reach for the letter opener and open this one first. Out fell a beautiful painting of the sun in glorious shades of yellow and orange. It had a huge toothy smile and the eyes were large blue pools of paint with glitter twinkles.

Sara read the words at the bottom.

To Aunty Sara,
Thank you for giving me my daddy for a whole month.
Love, Bonny
XXX

A few simple, heartfelt words of a child quickly brought a smile to Sara's face. Dear little Bonny with all her problems had thought to send such a beautiful painting to say thank you.

'Marjorie, isn't this the most wonderful picture you've ever seen?' Sara asked, proudly holding up the brightly coloured sheet of paper.

'Magnificent, Sara. Simply magnificent. We'll have to put it up on the pinboard in the waiting room.'

'Just be careful how you attach it to the wall,' she warned. 'I'll be taking this masterpiece with me when I go and I don't want it to tear.'

It took some time rearranging the other notices to accommodate such a big painting but finally it was done.

'Bonny's painting is like taking the sun out of the sky and having it in the room with us. It's just glorious,' Marjorie commented, stepping away to admire the decoration.

'Lucky she doesn't have her father's artistic ability.'

The voice made both women spin around in surprise. They hadn't heard the door open.

'Stu couldn't paint to save his life,' Tom added, before leaving both women and walking into his office.

There had been no 'Hello' or 'How are you?' No greeting whatsoever. Sara thought he must have decided to keep his distance after their words the previous night. She had such mixed emotions. She was upset with herself for being so rude but justified her lack of manners as a necessity to keep Tom at bay.

'What are you doing here, Tom?' she called as she followed after him.

He looked her up and down in an irritated silence. 'No food going cold? So you have time to talk today?' His eyes dropped down to the drawer of the filing cabinet that he was rummaging through.

'I was tired and cold—' she began.

'And just a little rude,' he continued for her.

Sara closed the office door and crossed to him. 'Fine,

I'm sorry. But, be fair, you've had bad days in the past and been less than gracious.'

'When?'

It was an honest question as Tom had never been rude to her in that way. They had disagreed, heaven knows how many times, but he had never been cruel or cold the way she had been to him.

'Point taken. I'm sorry for the way I behaved.' She walked to the window and stared outside in silence. She didn't want to tell him about her feelings as it wouldn't change anything. She just had to hope they would fade in time.

Suddenly she felt his warm hands kneading the soft flesh of her shoulders. She flinched and had to stifle a gasp. He stood so close behind her, his supple fingers finding the knots of tension and working them into putty. His masculine scent invaded her senses, sending red heat rushing to her cheeks and then flowing through her entire body.

'I can understand. I guess I threw you in at the deep end here, you must be exhausted.'

His hands on her body felt so good but she had no intention of letting him know that. She mustered a laugh, 'I never liked that briefcase anyway and you did ambush me somewhat.'

Tom smiled in spite of himself and gently turned her around to face him. They were so close. His soft lips, only inches from hers, were so inviting. She hated it that she wanted to taste him and hold him like she had that night a few weeks ago, and all those years before.

'I'd better be going,' he told her huskily, pulling his own feelings into check. 'You've got a full afternoon at the hospital.'

Without saying another word, Tom left.

Relieved that he had gone, Sara collapsed into the chair. She was so glad that she hadn't given in to her desire to kiss him. Just being near him and not reacting to him was so difficult, but she was determined to break through those feelings. She just wasn't sure how.

Taking a deep breath, Sara walked back into her office and gathered up her notes and X-rays for the afternoon's surgery at the hospital.

As Tom left the building he rushed to fill his lungs with the cold air. He had not realised touching Sara would stir feelings so quickly. He was doing his best to remind himself she was leaving and he needed to accept that they had no future together. There was no reason for her to stay. Nothing had changed. They both saw their lives laid out so differently. Sara saw the picket fence and a house filled with children, and he saw his life filled with work. Having children was not in his plans. He couldn't change and she shouldn't change. He loved her for being the loving, caring woman she was and it would be wrong to tie her to a life that gave her less than everything she wanted. Everything she deserved.

Sara drove to the hospital and then parked her car in the doctors' car park and made her way to the doctors' lounge on the fourth floor. It was adjacent to the oral and maxillofacial ward. She placed some groceries she had bought at the market on the way to the hospital in the refrigerator, relieved she would have a nice home-cooked meal for that evening. Fresh King George whiting and some vegetables to steam. She couldn't stomach the thought of takeaway again.

With her dinner safely tucked away, she headed up

to Theatre. She scrubbed and gowned and entered to find her drowsy patient already prepared for surgery.

'Hi, David, I'm Sara and, as Marjorie informed you over the phone, I will be carrying out today's procedure. If things go as smoothly as I envisage, you will be in Recovery in a little under two and a half hours with a brand-new-looking jaw but a bit of a sore hip for a few days.'

David smiled limply and tried to nod.

'After that you will be in ICU overnight and then off to a ward for another few days.'

'We're ready, Sara,' the theatre sister told her.

'Count slowly back from ten, David,' the anaesthetist said, and after a few moments David drifted off to sleep under the brilliant theatre lights. The nurse draped David in sterile green sheeting and prepared the surgical sites with antiseptic solution.

Sara checked the X-rays again on the viewer and then looked over towards the surgical trays nearby. 'Today we'll be undertaking a chin augmentation of this young man. We start with an intra-oral incision extending from canine to canine.' There was a first-year intern present so she briefed him on the procedure. 'I am aware of the risk to the long root apexes of the canine teeth and the associated nerve so will move cautiously.'

The operation took just over three hours. There was a short break when David was taken off to Recovery. The staff then rescrubbed and in fresh gowns and caps they returned for another three operations. The first was the release of an adult tongue-tie, followed by removal of the remaining upper and lower teeth of an elderly patient in preparation for full dentures, and the last was a complicated lower-jaw reduction and rhinoplasty. It was almost seven o'clock when they finished and the last young woman was wheeled into Recovery.

Sara thanked the staff for their skilled assistance. She then changed into her street clothes and visited the two patients in ICU, before dropping into the wards and checking the two other less serious cases. They were all progressing well. Sara reassured the concerned families that the patients all looked bruised and swollen but they were fine and then she decided to have a quick cup of coffee before heading home. She was almost dead on her feet after seven straight hours of surgery.

She had just sat down in the doctors' lounge, savouring the wonderful aroma of steaming coffee in her mug, when Tom and another doctor appeared, apparently in search of similar refreshment.

'Jake, have you met Sara? She's been kind enough to fill in for Stu while he's up on the farm.'

Sara watched as the man shook his head and walked towards her with his hand outstretched. She purposely avoided eye contact with Tom. She also noted that he hadn't referred to their relationship or history at all. She was just there to help out.

'Jake Manning, I'm in reconstructive surgery,' he told her. 'Pleased to meet you.'

'Likewise,' she told him, as she met his handshake. 'Please forgive me not standing up, but I'm done in. I've just finished a killer of an afternoon list.'

'I can appreciate how you're feeling,' he answered, and collapsed into the chair beside her, throwing his feet onto the low coffee table. 'I've had it for the day and I've only been on rounds.'

'I suppose this means I have to get the coffee,' Tom complained in jest.

Sara's eyes darted to and from Tom as he made his

way to the percolator. She tried not to stare, but the sight of his lithe body in form-fitting black linen trousers and an apricot-coloured cotton shirt was more appealing than ever.

'Sugar and white?' he enquired of his colleague.

'No, black and strong. I have a long drive home and I'll need something to keep me awake.'

'Why were the rounds so difficult today?' Sara asked as she lifted her feet up and curled them inside the chair and took another sip of her coffee. 'Heavy load or difficult patients?'

'No, that nervy intern by the name of—'

'Johnson!' Tom cut in smiling, as he crossed the room and placed the mugs heavily on the low table. 'I wondered where he'd turn up. Not that I made any enquiries, mind you.'

'That guy can talk,' Jake continued, reaching for his cup and cradling it in his hands. 'Actually, that's all he did. Talk and talk and—' Jake suddenly started slinking down in his seat. 'Don't look now, but speaking of the devil.'

The door was pushed open by a dishevelled Johnson. He looked around the room and then spied the three of them in the far corner.

'Dr Fielding, I'm sorry to bother you, I know you've finished for the day but your patient Mr Kowalski, the one who went missing and then we located him inadvertently exposing himself to the florists...'

Sara's eyes widened as she heard him recall the story. She watched him fidget nervously and then dig his hands into his white examination-coat pockets. He drew closer and sat down on the edge of the seat. 'You don't mind if I sit, do you?'

Sara leant forward and placed her mug on the table.

'Not at all. And by the way, I'm Sara, I'm filling in for Stu Anderson.'

'Oh, hi. I remember you from the other day in Dr Fielding's office. I hope your knee's okay. I'm so sorry about that. I guess I came across like a bit of a twit, I mean losing a patient and then crashing into you. I mean, it doesn't happen all that often. Actually, only twice this year, and the other one wasn't really missing, I mean, Mrs Summers died and she was taken to the morgue but no one told me. One of those admin types of problems, well, actually it was a heart problem, but then Admin didn't tell me…'

Tom dropped his cup onto the table. 'Johnson, please get to the point, it's getting late and we all want to go home. Is our patient all right?'

'Yes, Dr Fielding. It's just that Mr Kowalski doesn't have any family. He told me that his wife died about ten years ago and then the business went under. They never had any children and he lost contact with his brother, Alexander. I guess he was too embarrassed to admit that he had lost everything. He's been living in shelters on and off for the last nine years. So I would like to refer him to the social worker tomorrow, if that's okay.'

'That sounds like a good idea.'

He stood up, smiling, and backed out of the room. 'Thank you, Dr Fielding. I'll arrange it now.' And with that he was gone.

'Glad he's in your ward more often than mine,' Jake said with a smirk. 'He tries so hard I'd go mad!'

Tom leant forward and tapped his knees like a drum kit. 'He's a good kid but I think he could talk underwater. Some days it does wear thin.'

Sara stood up, smoothed her skirt and self-consciously

made her way to the sink. She wasn't sure if Tom was watching her but she felt like she was on show.

'So, Tom,' Jake began. 'I'm not giving up on the whole double-dating idea. I know you keep refusing but I have this amazing woman for you, and I can set it up on Saturday if you'd like. She's Bella's friend over from Adelaide. Pretty girl, radiologist, single....'

The sound of Sara's cup crashing onto the sink and sliding into the soapy water cut short Jake's words.

'Are you okay?' he asked.

'Tired, that's all. Like I said, it was a tough day.'

Sara wiped the suds from her clothes and concentrated on quickly washing and drying her cup. Tom lowered his voice and Sara was grateful that he did. She didn't need to hear his response but she heard Jake's answer.

'Think you're making a huge mistake, Tom. She's a great girl. Maybe next time, then.'

Sara was relieved. She wanted Tom to date, she really did, but she just wanted him to do it after she left Melbourne. When she was living in San Antonio, not now, not while she was still living next door. That would be too much to deal with.

Everything put away, she went to the fridge to collect her groceries.

'Oh, no! Where's it gone?' she exclaimed.

'Where's what?' Tom asked bluntly.

'My shopping bag, everything I bought for dinner. It's gone. Someone's walked off with it!'

Sara wasn't sure she was doing the right thing accepting Tom's dinner invitation but she was too tired to argue. He had offered to cook her a steak and she wasn't about to refuse. In fact, she was so hungry and exhausted that she would have eaten drive-through hamburgers and fries if Tom hadn't offered to cook dinner at her place.

She'd followed him home and on the way they had picked up some fresh bread from the continental deli. Tom had clinched the dinner deal with the promise of ice cream and hot chocolate sauce for dessert. He had run into his place and picked up the steaks while Sara unlocked her door and turned the lights on.

She told herself that she would simply enjoy Tom's company and, more particularly, the meal. To refuse would appear rude and also admit to both of them that she perhaps didn't trust herself to be alone with him.

'I'll throw the steaks under the grill,' he told her. 'Won't take too long. Why don't you turn the heater on and make yourself comfortable in the sitting room.'

'Because I can't turn the heater on.'

Tom gave a wry smile as he popped his head around the kitchen door. 'That's right, I forgot. I'll be right there.'

The bright light from the kitchen filtered through so she didn't bother to switch on a lamp. Tom lit the heater and they both returned to the kitchen to cook the steaks. Sara noticed how he knew where everything was, almost as if it was his kitchen. It was an odd level of familiarity, she thought, then she reminded herself that it was the reverse of their old home so it made sense that the kitchens would be the same.

Tom finished seasoning the steaks and put them on to cook. Together they prepared their meal and Sara felt so happy. She was enjoying Tom's company and trying her best to find a way to define their relationship in her mind. To find a suitable box in which to put them. Unfortunately she couldn't find a label to fit. Nothing came to mind with the feelings she still had.

The meal was wonderful and Tom had opened a nice Cabernet Sauvignon from the Hunter Valley. It was a smooth red wine that complemented the food but Sara declined, preferring a mineral water. Wine made her feel tired and she was already struggling to stay awake.

They talked about work and the cases she had seen over the last few days while they ate their ice cream, sitting together on the comfy sofa. Hours passed like minutes and they both relaxed like old times, each choosing to avoid the subject of children. They accepted in that area they would simply never agree. Then the subject of Bonny arose.

'Isn't Bonny's painting beautiful?'

Tom nodded as he took his last sip of wine and put the empty glass on the coffee table. 'Stu rang yesterday, actually, and apparently Bonny's coming along well. Better than anyone expected. She's not talking yet, she's still using a board to point to the letters of simple words, but they're confident her speech will return in a short while.'

Sara thoughtfully fingered the rim of her empty water glass. 'It must be terrible for them. I know how I would feel if she were mine. I'd be devastated—'

'Yes, I suppose you would,' he cut in. There was no bitterness in his voice, a touch of melancholy perhaps, but none of his signature hostility on the subject of children.

Tom reached across the table and affectionately brushed away the wisps of hair that were threatening to cover Sara's eyes. Her beautiful eyes. He felt sure that if they had children, they would all have those beautiful big blue eyes…

She flinched and bit the inside of her cheek. With his hand so close it was making her pulse quicken again.

Tom looked into her eyes. He needed to be honest with Sara. He knew that in order for them to find some sort of closure as their marriage ended, there should be no more unanswered questions between them. She had been honest with him about her parents and now she deserved the same. He decided it was the right time to share something with her. To let her know why he would never have children and that his decision was final. He suddenly felt safe to tell her now. To open up to her, secure in the knowledge that she would not try to change his mind. Her new life was waiting and their life together had ended a long time ago.

'Sara,' he began, 'I want to share something with you. I need you to finally understand why we are where we are. Why you're moving on and I choose to devote my life to work and not a family. You need to know. I owe it to you and I owe it to us and what we had together. I should have told you a long time ago.'

Sara was taken aback and her surprise wasn't masked. Her body shifted a little on her chair and she gently pulled her hands free from his. His desire to open up seemed so sudden. This was what she had wanted all along but he had never been prepared to do so. She was confused why he had decided to open up now. She suddenly felt the need to protect herself from what she was about to hear. She didn't know why.

'Go on,' she said, looking at Tom and his new serious expression.

'My brother Heath and I…' Tom started, then he stopped, choking on his words momentarily. 'Well, when we were young, and through until teenagers, we were mad keen on BMX bikes. It was our obsession but he was so much better than I was. He was an extremely skilled rider.'

Sara nodded. This information was nothing new. She was aware that Heath had been the under sixteen BMX state champion for Victoria at one time.

Tom cleared his throat. This was as difficult as he'd imagined. The guilt he felt was still so raw. So many years had passed and yet he could picture it all as if it were yesterday. Each time he thought about his actions it was the same regret that filled his mind and ripped at his heart. He wished he could travel back in time and change it all. Change everything. Relive his life and not be the irresponsible kid who had made a bad decision and ruined his brother's life. And consequently ruined his own chance of happiness with Sara.

'Heath was almost sixteen and I was fourteen,' he started with a sigh. 'He was at the qualifying event for the UCI BMX world championships. He just had to beat the last rider from the Gold Coast in order to win the top spot. I suggested a move that would set him apart. It was called a tail whip. It was risky but I urged him on and told him if he pulled it off he would be on his way to the next world championships. Only he didn't pull it off. He fell. And he was badly injured.'

'Oh, no.' Sara sat up. 'What happened to him?'

'Along with the broken collar bone and multiple abrasions, he suffered testicular trauma or, to be specific, testicular torsion. Long story short, no fatherhood for him.' Tom's face was contorted with guilt as he looked down at the floor. 'So how can I just go ahead and have a big happy family while he is left alone?'

Sara felt so sorry for Heath and for Tom. Both brothers' lives had been changed for ever by normal teenage behaviour that had gone wrong. It hadn't been malicious or even reckless. Sara thought adventurous was a better description. But she felt Tom was carrying a burden that wasn't his to carry.

'But accidents happen to good people every day, Tom, you know that as a doctor. Sometimes no one's to blame.'

'In this case there was. Me.'

'I know what you're saying and I feel desperately sorry for your brother but you were fourteen and you couldn't have known the repercussions.' Sara could see the pain in Tom's eyes and hear the sadness in his voice. It ripped at her heart to see his burden and to know he had been carrying this for so long. She wished he had confided in her before.

'Maybe not, but why should I walk away scot free?'

'You choosing not to have children is not going to change anything for your brother except rob him of the chance to be an uncle. And you are punishing yourself for something that happened decades ago,' she said, reaching for his hands. 'I wish you hadn't kept it from me. I wish you'd told me this years ago.'

'I couldn't because I knew you would try to make me see things your way.'

'Did you ever tell Heath about your decision?' she asked. 'I don't know him that well, we only spent a short time together, but he seemed so lovely. He's a kind, intelligent man who wouldn't expect you to give up your chance for a family. Does he even know that you made this sacrifice, and are continuing to make it years later?'

Tom looked away. 'There's no need for him to know. We're just two brothers who didn't have kids. That's it. He's never questioned me and I haven't seen the need to discuss it with him. He's still paying the price. Why should I be any different?'

'Because you're hurting more than just yourself in the process.' Sara hesitated and then decided to be more honest than she'd thought she ever would. 'You're hurting me and the children that we will never bring into this world because of your decision.'

Tom lips tightened. He knew she was right. And he didn't want to hurt her. He hated it that he couldn't give her everything in the world she wanted. But he couldn't. He knew she would be better off without him.

'This is exactly why I didn't tell you.'

'But you were a child, you were fourteen. You can't own that guilt for ever. It's not fair to you. And I don't think Heath would want you to own it for ever,' Sara argued.

'Heath's marriage ended because of the accident. They tried IVF for years unsuccessfully and it wore them down. He never told anyone but me. How can I look past that? I caused that pain. I wrecked his chance for a happy marriage and children of his own. That's not something that happened when we were kids, Sara, it happened three years ago.'

Sara looked at the man sitting opposite her and she suddenly saw a very different man. He wasn't a selfish, career-driven man who disliked children at all. He was a man who had put his needs last. It was so sad and ironic that she finally putting her needs first and Tom's decision to place his needs last was what had driven them apart. And yet she had never suspected anything even close to that. She had thought the very opposite for more than three years.

She knew more than ever that he would always own her heart and now she needed to somehow get through to him. To make him see that he was throwing away a future with his own children and this sacrifice, however noble, wouldn't change anything. It would only seal their fate.

CHAPTER EIGHT

SARA AWOKE AND rubbed her eyes as she slowly rose from the softness of her warm pillow. She thought back to the night before. They had talked for hours. She had tried desperately to change Tom's mindset. She had pleaded with him to talk to Heath. To be honest about wanting children and apologise again for what happened but explain that they all needed to move on. Move past the hurt and the blame and find a way to be in each other's lives and accept the past.

Although Tom had seen how it was hurting Sara too, he felt in his heart he had made the right decision. It was in his eyes the only course of action. He had made a decision over twenty years ago and he wasn't going back on it. Sara had felt helpless to change his mind when he'd finally left in the early hours of the morning.

She realised she must have fallen into the deepest sleep when she turned and looked at the clock beside the bed. It was seven-thirty. She remembered talking and trying to make Tom see the situation from the outside. She remembered crying a few times too. The accident was a secret that Tom and Heath had kept from her. She had never met her brother-in-law's wife—both times she had stayed in the US while Heath had headed out to Australia to visit. Perhaps it was because she had been undergoing the IVF treatments or perhaps because they had been struggling within the marriage. Sara realised she would never know.

Tom had decided he had a cross to bear for something he'd innocently done as a child, something he felt he had to take responsibility for the rest of his life. She wished there was a way she could get through to him. Sara knew she loved Tom and even though their marriage was over she knew she would never stop caring.

She hoped, not for her sake but for Tom's, that he would one day see it differently. At fourteen, she knew only too well that boys thought they were invincible. She imagined Tom and Heath thought the same way. The idea that one adventurous BMX trick could go horribly wrong and affect the rest of their lives would have been incomprehensible to both of them.

Sara knew it was going to be almost impossible to try to sway Tom's opinion at this time. It was strange but she finally felt now, with this understanding of Tom's attitude and behaviour, that she knew him more intimately than she had ever known him before. This was the real Tom. The caring man who would not turn his back on what he perceived as the permanent scars he had inflicted on his brother. He was a hero, but unfortunately he was a misguided hero. And she had no idea how, or even if, she could change his direction.

She still felt a little tired. Her eyes had been so heavy the night before and they were no different this morning. It was out of character for her to be this exhausted and if it continued, she decided she would have some blood work done. It had been a struggle to get through the day and she'd slept so soundly when her head had hit the pillow. This level of tiredness had occurred once before and it had been anaemia. An iron supplement, spinach or red meat, she decided, might be the order of the day until her count was back up again.

Sara rolled on her back, drawing in a deep breath before she slowly exhaled. In silence, she studied the pattern of the pressed iron ceiling, not really seeing it. The night before had been as enlightening as it had been frustrating. The conversation they had shared had been the most honest they had ever been with each other. Tom had finally opened up to her, and she assumed he found it easier now they were close to finalising the divorce. It was too late for both of them and perhaps it made it less painful for him. She knew his deepest secret but was almost powerless to sway him to choose with his heart. His misguided conscience had ruled his head for far too long.

'Hello…anyone awake?'

Sara jumped at the sound of Tom's voice from the other side of the wall.

'I'm awake and just getting up,' she called back loudly.

'I made breakfast. I've just eaten mine but I have some for you if you'd like to unlock the door. The key's on the dresser.'

Sara had noticed the internal door that linked the two homes but assumed it had been locked for years. She climbed from bed and searched the dresser.

'Not here, I'm afraid,' she called back, slightly pleased there was no key and no way for Tom to be in her bedroom.

'Try the top drawer on the left, it might be in there.'

Sara sighed. He wasn't giving up. How did he know where everything was? She decided not to think too much of it. He was an organised person. She pulled the drawer open and found a neat stack of men's summer T-shirts. She assumed they were Tom's. Then she felt at the bottom of the drawer and found a set of keys.

'Got them.' She couldn't lie. She also had to let him in. With reservations, Sara unlocked the door and opened it to see Tom, still in his dressing gown, smiling at her with a breakfast tray held high. She stepped back, allowing him to enter.

'After the last fall Mrs Vanderbilt had, just before she had to be admitted to the nursing home, she wanted to know I could get through to help in an emergency. So she gave me the key,' he said. 'Made her feel more secure knowing she had someone close by to help in an emergency.'

It didn't give Sara anywhere near the same feeling as she eyed the doorway suspiciously. Her version of ground rules for their working relationship did not extend to her soon-to-be-ex-husband being able to access her bedroom day and night. It may have been a comforting thought for Mrs Vanderbilt but it was definitely was not a comforting thought for *her.*

'Anyway, I thought you might like this to start the day.' He crossed the room and placed a tray of hot coffee and a piece of toast on the bedside table. 'Don't want you feeling bad on your day off because I kept you up talking way too late last night.'

Feeling chilly, Sara climbed back into bed and pulled the covers up.

Tom was feeling anxious about the conversation they'd shared and he wanted to see firsthand that in the light of day Sara accepted his decision was not negotiable. Her newfound knowledge of the reason why he would not consider having children would never change it. His mind was made up. He took full responsibility for the accident and equally the end of his brother's marriage.

There was no other way to see it. And nothing she could say would change anything.

'You have a full day of surgery tomorrow, so rest up.' He walked over to open the curtains and thought better of it. 'Maybe we'll leave these closed and you can stay in bed for a while after breakfast. Take your time and read a book or something.'

'Tom,' Sara began, 'about last night.'

'Sara, let's not go there,' he said, turning back to face her. 'I said what I should have told you before we married. It was my fault for thinking children wouldn't be an issue. We never talked seriously about having them or not having them. I guess I assumed being just the two of us for ever would be okay with you. No doubt you, on the other hand, thought I would warm to the idea of having kids. It's my fault completely for rushing you to the altar.'

Sara's lips curved to a melancholy smile. It had been a crazy courtship. She had been excited and had never really thought too far ahead. She had been marrying the man she loved. The man she admired and respected and thought would naturally be the father of her children.

'I'm sad that now I know the truth I still can't change your mind, Tom. I think you would be the most wonderful father and I feel certain that you and Heath could work through everything if only you would speak with your brother. Tell him how you feel and see how he feels. He may have no idea that you are still carrying this guilt. He may even have moved on and assumed you've done the same. I know he would want you to be happy.'

'And I want you to be happy, Sara. It's all I've ever

wanted, but talking to my brother won't change anything. What's done is done.'

Tom swallowed hard and asked her to leave the subject alone. He was glad he had finally opened up but he didn't want to go over the past any more. Sara just had to accept his decision and he would accept her decision to each travel a different path. He wanted with all of his heart for the ending to be different but it couldn't be. They might be heading in opposite directions but there were another few weeks yet to spend together and that made him happy in a bittersweet way. He leant down and helped to plump up her pillow before he picked up the breakfast tray and placed it on her lap.

'I'll get ready and head off to the hospital, but you should enjoy your day off. I have lectures all day at the university and then marking to do at the hospital tonight so I'll be late home and probably won't see you till tomorrow. Oh, and by the way, the local grocery store down the road is still there. You might like to stock the fridge if you're low on anything. Still the same old family business it was when you were here and they still make the best rock cakes ever.'

Tom smiled and left the room the way he had come in, shutting the door behind him. He felt like a weight had lifted from him. Although he also recognised that when Sara did move on, marry and have a family, it would be difficult to stay in contact. The thought of her waking in another man's arms and sharing a life with her new husband and children would be too much for him to handle.

While Sara sat and ate her breakfast she tried to process all that Tom had told her. After a night to think about it, she felt no less frustrated. At least she now knew the man she had married a little better. She knew now that Tom wasn't selfish. In fact, he was a man of great principles. Although principles wouldn't keep him warm at night or throw their arms around his neck when they came rushing home from school. He was certainly sacrificing a lot for his brother.

Short of a miracle and Tom seeing the light, there wasn't a lot she could do but accept Tom's decision. Thankfully the day went by smoothly. She had made a few phone calls and organised for some of the boxes of clothes she had packed for Texas to be forwarded to Melbourne. She walked down to the local grocer's and stocked the refrigerator and pantry, picking up some rock cakes as well.

Sara left one in a bag by Tom's front door.

She spent the afternoon with her feet up, reading through some notes for the next day's surgical cases. Then she watched some daytime television, cooked an omelette for dinner and soaked in a long bubble bath.

Once she was snug back in her own pyjamas, she locked the door between the adjoining houses, slipped back under the covers and drifted into a restful sleep.

On Friday she arrived early at the hospital. She had a long day's surgical list. The morning was filled with two of Tom's private patients. The afternoon with Stu's. They were all straightforward and she was keen to start. That evening she had an appointment at the practice with George and his mother, so she wanted to get away on time.

There was a break at around one, between lists, so Sara went up to the doctors' lounge to close her eyes and put her feet up for a bit.

'Hello, Sara.'

Sara opened her eyes to see Tom standing in front of her. 'Hi, there, stranger,' she managed in a cool tone. 'On your lunch break?'

He sat down. 'No, I've finished up for the day. It's the first day of the mid-year break for the students so no lectures or rotations to organise for the rest of the week. Although I'm not a great believer in the current lecture model anyway,' he announced with a frustrated sigh. 'I think we need to bring changes to medical student education, bring it up to speed by actually reducing the number of lectures.'

Sara could see he felt quite passionate about this subject. 'Go on,' she urged him, as she sipped her chocolate milk.

He turned and faced her. She couldn't help but notice his eyes light up as he spoke. He was so animated. She remembered he always was when he felt strongly about something. 'Let's face it, there have been huge changes in the world of medicine but medical education has remained the same. We're in a time warp and I don't think we're keeping up with student needs or expectations. There's been growth in information and research in all facets of medicine. Yet we keep delivering the traditional lecture style of teaching, despite class attendance falling and complaints that we're failing to produce compassionate, well-trained medicos.'

Sara nodded, agreeing with Tom's valid argument for change.

'We need to make better use of the time we're given to train doctors. I'd like to see lecture content delivered differently. Perhaps in short videos that are watched by the students in their own time, and as often as they need, to ensure they grasp the concepts and really understand the material. Class time is then freed up for focusing on patients' clinical stories as a way to apply this medical information.'

Sara was impressed as always with Tom's knowledge and passion. She knew his new role as associate professor was well deserved. He was no doubt going to make a difference at the hospital. She only wished she could be there to see the changes he made and the real outcomes for the students and the patients. She was so proud of the man she'd married and the man, she knew in her heart, she would always love.

'And now I will climb down from my soapbox,' he said with a laugh, sitting back a little and relaxing. 'I have papers to assess but other than that this week is a good one for me. I get to take a breather.'

'Some people get all the luck,' Sara sighed. 'I've got a full list for Stu and then an appointment back at the practice at about seven.'

'What if I assist?' Tom suggested, as he sat upright again and rubbed his chin thoughtfully. 'Then you can get through it even quicker.'

Sara considered Tom's suggestion for a moment. In the past, working with Tom had always been the highlight of her day. Watching the skill of the man who had inspired her and taught her so much had always been an honour, so with a nod of her head she agreed to share the operating theatre for one last time. She knew she hadn't forgotten his operating style—in fact, it was almost hers. He had been the best teacher and mentor she could have asked for as a student. If she wanted to move past their lives as husband and wife and begin again as colleagues, she needed to start now.

'I'd like that.' She smiled.

* * *

Sara was ready and waiting in Theatre when Tom appeared in the scrub room.

'Afternoon, people,' he said, as he crossed to the operating table. He looked down at the teenage boy who was at this stage already a little groggy. 'I bet you're feeling more than a bit nervous, Matt, but listen, mate, there's absolutely nothing to worry about. During the surgery we're going to bring that jaw of yours into a respectable position, and while we're at it reshape your chin a bit. You won't be able to keep the girls away after we've finished with you. But don't worry, before you leave the hospital we'll provide you with a large stick to beat them away!'

Sara smiled to herself. He was incorrigible. But that was part of his charm.

She loved the way he communicated so naturally with patients of any age. He never played the academic with his patients. He was so down to earth. She also noticed that in Theatre she was an equal. He paid her no special attention.

'Any questions before we start?' he asked. 'That's not just from you, Matt. Any questions from the crew?'

They all shook their heads as they went about their respective jobs within the operating theatre.

'Okay, Matt, you're off to sleep, mate. See you in a few hours.'

The anaesthetist took over and Matt drifted out of consciousness.

Sara and Tom worked well together. Neither had changed their approach to the operation and four skilled hands made it a relatively easy procedure.

Sara screwed the first titanium plate in place.

'Damn, I taught you well,' Tom commented lightheartedly to Sara, but all the while appreciating her level of skill. He felt a sense of pride as he watched her dexterity with the complex surgical procedure.

She smiled but didn't raise her eyes. They completed fifteen minutes ahead of time. Tom left promptly to read up on the next patient.

The entire afternoon went as smoothly. Working with Tom, Sara remembered why she had chosen oral and maxillofacial surgery as her specialty. She had watched his fingers perform magic in the operating theatre and she had been mesmerised. Not just by the tall, handsome tutor—it was his talent and love of his work that had inspired her to follow the same path.

They finished the last of the patients around five-thirty, which gave Sara plenty of time to change, pick up something to eat and be at the practice to meet with the other post-operative patients before George arrived. She crossed her fingers that George would show up and be prepared to listen to the other boys.

As she buttoned up her coat, her mobile phone began ringing.

'Hello, Sara Fielding.'

'Sara, it's Marjorie. I'm afraid I have some bad news.'

Sara frowned as she slipped her hair behind her ear to hear better. 'What is it, Marjorie?'

'Both boys who were coming along to talk to George. They've cancelled.'

'What, both of them?'

'Yes, apparently some heavy steel band, Slayer, I think she called them, has stayed on in Melbourne for a second concert and they're going. Neither were prepared to miss out.'

Sara collapsed back into the chair despondently. 'They're a heavy *metal* band, but what am I going to do now? If I don't have those boys there by seven o'clock,

George will never agree to his surgery. Stu's patient will be living on a sheep station in the middle of nowhere by this time next week.'

Sara knew there was only one other person who could convince George to go ahead with the surgery. That would be Tom. She had wanted so desperately to handle the practice on her own and to prove that she was capable and had the capacity to deal with any issues that arose. But George had already shown signs of disapproving of her. More than likely, it was the general dismissive attitude of a sixteen-year-old boy. His mother had been on the receiving end too, as Sara had witnessed firsthand.

Sara knew this was no time for pride. This was Stu's patient and she needed to exhaust all avenues before she accepted that George would cancel his surgery, a decision she knew for certain he would regret as an adult.

Sara had only an hour and a quarter now to be at the practice. There was no point turning up alone. George would not listen to her.

Sara dialled Tom's mobile. George might listen to a man. Sometimes teenage boys thought more of another male's opinion. And Tom certainly had a way with patients. It was worth trying.

She wasn't sure if Tom was still in the hospital or if he had left.

Damn, he had switched his phone to voice mail. Sara left a message and asked him to meet her at the practice. She briefly explained the situation and its urgency because of George's plans to move up north to the sheep station. She hoped he would make it in time.

She grabbed her case and rushed out to the lift. With her head down, and in a hurry, she turned the corner and almost ran straight into Johnson.

'That was close,' he said, smiling. 'Almost *déjà vu*! Seems like you're in a hurry this time.'

'You have no idea. I don't have a spare minute. I've got a surgical patient due in a little over an hour at the practice—'

'But that's only fifteen minutes from here,' he cut in, reaching down to pick up her briefcase. 'You don't have to rush, unless of course you haven't eaten, then I suppose you would need the extra time, but there's a hospital cafeteria—'

'Johnson,' Sara cut in tersely, 'I'm afraid I don't even know your first name.'

'Nigel.'

'Thank you, Nigel,' Sara said, more than a little anxious about the unfolding situation. 'But I need to find Dr Fielding.'

'He's up in the lecture theatre, tidying up, I think. If you don't know where that is, I can show you.'

'That'd be great.'

Sara followed Nigel as he led her to another floor. 'Excuse me asking,' Nigel began, through a mouthful of muesli bar, 'but are you married to Dr Fielding or are you his sister?'

'No, we're married but separated. It's all very amicable,' she added.

Nigel nodded. 'I asked, because they were all talking about it in Theatre today. With your names, they didn't know if he was on his best behaviour for his sister or his wife.'

Sara gave a wry smile, knowing she and Tom were already the topic of hospital gossip. She followed Nigel till they reached the lecture theatre, where he left her at the open double doors.

Tom lifted his head, as if he sensed her near.

'You have more patients for me?' he asked with a smile.

'Not exactly, well, not at the hospital. This is one of Stu's private patients,' she answered, as she climbed down the stairs towards Tom at the front of the large tiered room.

'My skeletal class-three malocclusion, George Andrews, has cancelled his surgery for a number of reasons. But not one of them is valid,' Sara explained, as she drew closer. 'His friends have made him worried about the possibility of death or brain damage on the operating table and on top of that Mrs Andrews informs me that they've convinced him to head up north and work as a jackeroo, where his bite won't offend the sheep!'

Tom shook his head. 'Crazy kids.'

Sara smiled as he said it.

'And what can I do?'

Sara looked thoughtfully at Tom. 'I hoped you might be able to explain to him the repercussion of not proceeding with the surgery. I honestly think he's at that age when a man-to-man talk might serve him better.'

'I'm happy to tell it like it is to George and let him weigh up his choices and let him make his decision. I think it's our best shot.'

'Sounds like a plan.'

Tom stacked the last of the papers he had been gathering, put them in a large folder and scooped it under his arm. 'Let's do it, shall we?'

There was a knock on the practice door and Sara looked up to see Mrs Andrews in the waiting room with a very surly-looking George.

'Would you like to have a subtle word with George

out there while I keep his mother busy?' she whispered to Tom. 'I think the waiting room is less formal and intimidating.'

Tom took his cue and stood up and walked out into the waiting room. Casually he picked a car racing magazine before flopping into a chair.

'And what am I supposed to do?' George growled. 'Sit around while you both moan about me behind my back? I can't see why I even had to come. Complete waste of time, if you ask me!'

'Actually, George, I have to discuss a few things with your mother and I would like you to have a chat with Dr Fielding.'

Mrs Andrews anxiously entered the office and George sat down in the waiting room with an annoyed expression upon his face.

'I almost had to drag him here kicking and screaming,' Mrs Andrews confessed. 'There was some free concert thing on tonight—'

'And don't I know it,' Sara told her with a sigh as she closed the door on Tom and George.

'George, I'm Dr Fielding,' Tom said, as he dropped the magazine on the seat beside him. 'I thought we could have a chat about the surgery. I heard you've cancelled,' Tom went on as he moved to a chair closer to the young man.

George just looked up with a disinterested expression. 'Do you know how long my mum is gonna be? I wanna go already.'

'She's in there, talking to Sara, so I'm not sure. But I'd like to chat to you about your decision—'

'I'm not having it done any more,' he cut in rudely.

Tom lifted one eyebrow and rubbed the back of his

neck. 'Absolutely your choice, mate. But I'm not sure you're cancelling for the right reasons.'

'What do you mean?'

'Well, unless you have much older and wiser friends with medical backgrounds, then they're not qualified to discuss the risks or advantages of the surgery.'

'But I could die on the table.'

'You could die bungee-jumping or doing doughnuts in your car on a dirt road up north, but you'll probably do both with your friends.'

'Probably.' George was eyeing Tom suspiciously but now seemed to be listening. Clearly the doughnuts on the dirt road had rung true.

'Listen, George, the operation is not for the faint-hearted. I won't lie to you, but without it you will have much bigger problems in the long run. It's not about appearance. Even chewing will become more difficult with a jaw discrepancy like yours.'

'So I won't be able to eat a steak?'

'George, as you get older everything will become more difficult. You have to think down the track, not just today. Your long-term health needs to be considered. Even your nutritional needs and the effect on your digestive system needs to be considered. This might not mean a lot now but later you will find it difficult. Your friends won't be there then.'

'So it's not just for looks.'

'Absolutely not, George, although that is a bonus,' Tom said with a wink. 'Never hurts to look good for the ladies.'

Tom noticed George's body language relax and become less defensive.

'Maybe I'll think about it, then,' he announced.

'Can't ask you to do more than that. But don't go to

your friends for medical advice. I'm sure they know loads about the latest apps and games, but definitely not about surgical procedures.'

'Can you tell the doctor in with my mum that I'll think about it? I'll make up my mind in a couple of days.'

CHAPTER NINE

AFTER GEORGE AND Mrs Andrews left the office, Sara thanked Tom for his successful intervention. She knew he had a way with patients, particularly teenagers, and his inroads with George proved it. As they made their way to the car park, she asked Tom about an invitation she had received in the mail a few days earlier.

'By the way, have you rung Dana and Stu with your answer yet?' she asked as she opened her car door.

He paused with her door ajar. 'Answer to what? I haven't heard from them.'

'They sent us both letters asking us to be godparents to the twins. The christening is in two weeks.'

Tom didn't mask his confusion as he hopped into the Healey and wound down the old-fashioned window. 'Honestly, Sara, I have no idea what you're talking about. I'm aware there's the christening coming up but I haven't received anything from them. Typical of Stu, he probably just left it on my desk somewhere for me to find. I'll look tomorrow and get back to you. But I have to be honest, I'm not sure how I feel about being a godparent. All things considered, I don't think it's a good idea.'

'Tom, they're not asking us to adopt them. I think it's a wonderful idea.' Sara thought it was an honour and she was sorry that they had all drifted apart over the last few years. She was determined that would not happen again and she couldn't wait to catch up with Dana again. The prospect of being the boys' godmother made her happy. It meant that she would have strong links to their family for ever. This time in Melbourne had made her realise she didn't want to leave it all behind. She loved her friends and wanted to be a part of their lives.

'I'll think about it,' he told her flatly, before starting the car to drive home. *Think long and hard about it*, he told himself. Sara's car was soon an illuminated speck in his rear-vision mirror.

The next day went along steadily. Tom told her he would be working late at Augustine's. It was about one o'clock when Sara received a telephone call from the country. She had finished with the morning's patients and was enjoying a break with a hot mug of minestrone soup when the call came through.

'Sara, hi, it's Dana. How are you?'

Sara rested the cup down on the coaster Marjorie had given her. 'Dana, I'm well, really well,' she said, leaning forward onto the desk. 'But how are things going with you? How's Bonny coming along? It was just such a beautiful painting she sent me.'

'Thanks, I'll tell her you liked it. She's coming along so well, I can't tell you how grateful we are to you for stepping in and taking over.'

'Don't worry about that. I'm just glad I could help out.'

'We'll never forget it,' Dana said softly. 'It's made all the difference. And that's why I'm ringing. We hadn't heard back from you. Sara, Stu and I really want you to be their godmother. Bonny's done so well in only a week that we've decided to have a big party for Henry and Phillip's christening. We had planned on something low key but now practically the whole town is coming.

'Sara,' Dana's voice called down the line, 'please, don't feel pressured. I understand if you're too busy. Really, I don't want you to feel that you have to. We'd love to have you up for the party just as our guest. I'm sure Stu could ask someone else.'

'I'm not feeling pressured. Not at all. I'd be thrilled to be the boys' godmother, it's just that I'm not sure if Tom will agree. He's a bit hesitant—'

'That's wonderful!' Dana cut in. 'And don't worry about Tom. Stu spoke to him today and he's on board too. Gosh it's going to be so great to see you again. It's been so long and we have so much to catch up on.'

Sara nodded into the telephone. 'Yes, it will be great, really great,' she managed to reply, totally surprised at Tom's shift in attitude. What had made him change his mind? Was he coming round on some level to the idea of children after all? She realised every day just how complex Tom was and how he could still astonish her.

The afternoon was as steady as the morning. There were new patient consultations and a couple of post-operative checks.

'You certainly like to be busy, Sara,' Marjorie commented late in the day, as she placed the last of the typed reports on Sara's desk for her signature. 'You've booked a hectic surgical schedule for the next few weeks.'

'Marjorie, I'm fine. I'm not being paid to sit around and do nothing.'

'I know, but you must also look after yourself,' she said firmly. 'What about we close up and head off home? Your minor surgical list tomorrow is a long one.

Starts at eight o'clock and we won't finish much before six tomorrow evening. Laura and William North will be with us for the entire day.'

Sara agreed it was a good idea and gathered up her case notes for the next day's patients. She intended to read them briefly during the evening to refresh her memory. Locking the door, she headed downstairs.

Wistfully, Sara looked across the reflections in the river and for a moment her imagination took over and convinced her that she was heading home to spend the evening curled up with Tom instead of a pile of cold case notes. With the gas fire warming the room, she pictured Tom cuddling her as they sat together on the sofa, his arms wrapped tightly around her. But her fantasy slowly faded in the cold night air.

She came back to reality and the overwhelming loneliness of the deserted car park. Absent-mindedly, she rubbed her arms and shivered.

She knew she shouldn't allow her thoughts to wander to Tom. But thinking about him wasn't a conscious decision. No matter how hard she tried to block him from her mind, something would always remind her of him. And when she was by herself she needed no prompting to find his image creeping back in. He had unlocked the key to her heart many years ago and now, despite her protests, it appeared he had subtly crept back in.

Mollie Hatcher was on time the next morning and more than a little apprehensive about losing the gap between her front teeth.

'But my grandma says it's good luck to have a gap,' Mollie told them, her big brown eyes wide with worry.

Sara smiled understandingly. 'You know, Mollie, my grandma told me exactly the same story, and you never know—it might just be true. But it doesn't mean you have to keep the gap to keep the good luck! Especially not if it makes it hard to fit the rest of your teeth in and it stops them from meeting together properly.'

'I don't understand.'

'Well, your teeth came through with a gap. Now, if your grandma's story is true, then the good luck has already been decided for you. So there's no need to keep the gap.'

'I suppose,' she said, with a frown wrinkling the spattering of freckles on her nose. 'But will it hurt?'

'Mollie,' the anaesthetist interrupted softly, 'do you like butterflies?'

'Oh, yes, I love the big, bright coloured ones.'

William smiled. 'That's good, because I'm going to rub some special cream onto your hand and a butterfly is going to sit there and make you feel a bit sleepy. You'll still be awake and able to hear Sara and help her but you won't feel anything she does, so it won't hurt at all.'

The neuroleptanagesia quickly took effect, and Sara was able to remove the fleshy frenum that ran between Mollie's upper front teeth. She carefully sutured and then packed the site with a dressing before Laura helped the child into Recovery.

Following her appointment with Mollie, Sara's morning passed without incident—the minor surgical cases were straightforward and uneventful.

Sara's mind strayed to Tom. She hadn't seen much of him for a few days—the mid-year break was over and the hospital was monopolising his time. She had heard his car come and go at odd hours, but she had resisted the urge to pull back the drapes and peer out at him from the window. They had bumped into each other leaving for work, and Sara suggested shopping together for christening presents on the weekend. Tom seemed hesitant at first but then agreed and made a time for Saturday.

Sara had worried the day shopping would be fraught with tension but it was lovely and so far from her initial concerns. She had assumed the idea of buying presents for children would make Tom feel uncomfortable. But it didn't. Tom seemed happy enough to be looking at silver frames and other keepsakes but he had his own ideas too.

He suggested a large antique train set or racing cars as an alternative, then humoured Sara as she wandered around the delicate ornaments for about half an hour. After she asked the salesperson to reserve two stunning silver frames while she wandered a little more just to be sure of her purchase, he took Sara off to the toy department. She watched him for the first time roam around like a kid himself. He was wide-eyed and enthusiastic about what the boys would love now, and as they grew older. Which toys would be the most exciting, and how Stu could enjoy playing with the toys with his sons.

Sara felt a tug at her heart as she saw the genuine interest he had in finding something the children would love.

Finally he saw them. Two six-foot, enormous brown teddy bears.

'I'm not sure,' she said, looking up at the huge furry creatures. 'They're so big. I don't know where Dana would put them. Wouldn't it be nice to have something to keep?'

Tom nodded. 'If that's what you want, I guess you're right. We should be practical. Let's get the silver frames.'

Sara smiled. Shopping with Tom wasn't difficult at

all but it was sad seeing his reaction to the toys he would never share with his own children. She had the frames gift-wrapped and they headed off to enjoy lunch at a café before they left the city. Sara felt sure Dana would love the frames. Tom didn't say anything more but he really did love the bears.

Sara had less than two weeks left on her locum assignment for Stu.

George's surgery came around very quickly. She had called in to see him that night on the way home and gone over the procedure. He wanted the rhinoplasty as well and his mother was happy with that decision. Sara explained to George that he would be wearing anti-embolism stockings prior to his surgery and following the operation to reduce the possibility of deep vein thrombosis.

'Now, on top of everything else, I've gotta wear pantyhose?'

Sara smiled, 'No, George, not pantyhose. These are like thin white socks that compress your legs to increase the blood flow, preventing your leg veins from expanding. It stops blood pooling in your legs and forming a clot.'

He turned to his mother. 'Just make sure no one takes photos of me in the pantyhose-sock things. If that gets online I am so totally screwed.'

Sara slept well and was ready for a full day when she arrived at the hospital.

'Good morning, Rosalie.'

'Hi, Sara. Good to see you again,' the theatre nurse said, as Sara entered the scrub room. 'Long list again today.'

'Certainly is. Starts with George Andrews. He's understandably nervous. It's a long op he's looking at.' Dressed in her green theatre scrubs, with her hair secured under a surgical cap, Sara began lathering her hands and arms.

'If it goes as smoothly as last week,' Rosalie replied as she rinsed the lather from her hands and forearms, 'it'll be a dream for everyone.'

'Unfortunately we don't have Dr Fielding helping out, if that's what you mean—'

'Oh, yes, you do.' Tom's deep voice came from the other side of the small room.

Sara spun on her surgically booted heels to find him also dressed in theatre garb and scrubbing in at the opposite trough. He turned to face her at that exact moment.

'What are you doing here?' she asked. 'I have an assisting surgeon already confirmed.'

She soon found herself facing his broad back as he turned back round to rinse his hands. She watched in astonishment as he casually dried them and slipped into his latex gloves.

'Fran Burton, your assisting surgeon, just called Marjorie, who in turn called my office to say she had been held up and would be late. Great excuse to take a break from paperwork, so I'll help with the first patient and she'll be here to take over in time for number two.'

Tom had more than enough to occupy his time but he'd jumped at the opportunity to work with Sara again.

'Great,' she replied, a little surprised he hadn't just sent another resident surgeon to help. 'Let's get going.'

George was prepped and already in Theatre. The anaesthetist and two nurses were also waiting under the bright lights.

'Hi, George,' Sara greeted his anxious face. 'I won't ask you how you're feeling. I can pretty much guess the answer. But everything will be fine—'

'You don't happen to have a hip flask in your pocket now, do you? I could really do with something to take the nerves away.'

Tom laughed. 'Dr North has something even stronger planned for you. So, if you're ready, let's get started.'

George nodded and William administered the anaesthetic. The patient, groggier by the moment, began slowly counting backwards from ten. By seven he was asleep.

Tom let Sara lead the operation. He backed her up and anticipated each of her moves. She was so happy to have him working with her.

Once she had freed George's lower jaw, she removed an equal portion from the right and left sides. Tom assisted by securing the newly sized jaw with titanium plates. They worked steadily and advanced the midsection of his upper jaw. Next was the reshaping of the chin, and then they moved up to his nose. The bump was removed and after three hours the operation was complete. By all indications it was a success.

Sara had felt like she was in possession of four hands. Their chatter was minimal as each knew the other's next move, both equally skilled in the operating theatre.

Sara wished Tom would stay for the entire day. Fran was a more than capable surgeon but Tom just happened to be extraordinary. Yet professional courtesy wouldn't have her decline Fran's assistance.

'Thanks for your help,' she said to Tom as they watched George wheeled away into Intensive Care. 'It went extremely well.'

Tom considered her in silence. She felt uncomfortable as his eyes lingered on her face. She wondered what he was thinking. Was he considering her surgical skills or looking at her as a woman?

'We make an outstanding team, Sara,' he finally said. 'Texas is lucky to be getting you.' With that he bent down and tenderly kissed her cheek. He smiled sadly at her as he tugged the surgical gloves from his hands and walked away, leaving Sara standing alone in the empty theatre.

CHAPTER TEN

ICU's BUSTLING AMBIENCE of sterile efficiency was unusually sombre when Sara visited after finishing her surgical list for that day. It was around seven o'clock. All but one of her patients had been admitted to a high-dependency ward after Recovery. But it was policy for the more complicated cases to spend a night in ICU.

Each of the critical care patients had an attending nurse but the faces of their carers showed little emotion as they efficiently went about their work.

The silence was broken only by mechanical sounds: the unrelenting and regular high-pitched beeps of monitors; the constant buzzers; and the deep swooshing sound of the ventilators.

Pale blue curtains separated the patients whose acute medical conditions made their lives dependent upon sophisticated monitoring equipment and round-the-clock nursing. Each curtain was drawn open at the foot of the bed and the senior nurse at the desk had a clear view of each cubicle.

'Good evening, Vanda.' Sara's voice was little more than a whisper. 'I'm here to see George Andrews.'

'Evening, Sara,' the pretty nurse replied softly, before she drew a deep sigh and checked her list. 'George is in bed nine. He's doing very well. Debbie is looking after him tonight.'

'Has his mother been in?'

'She just left. Pretty horrified, by the look on her face. But Debbie and Dr Fielding put her at ease a bit and told her it looked a lot worse than it was.'

'Dr Fielding was here?'

'Yes,' the young nurse replied. 'He's still with him now.'

Sara wasn't surprised. Tom always treated his patients like family while they were in his care. The best care for each and every one of them. That obviously had not changed. Sara made her way over to George. He was sleeping. As expected, his jaw and cheeks were a harsh blend of bruises and quite swollen. His darkened eyes looked sunken in the puffiness of his face. He had been connected to a cardiac monitor and lines from intravenous bottles providing fluid, antibiotics and pain relief fed into his veins.

'Hello, Debbie, hello, Tom,' Sara said. 'I hear our patient is doing very well.'

'Hi, Sara,' Debbie replied. 'Yes, he's fine, but, then, we never expected any problems. His chart says his op was a reasonable length but straightforward. There's no reason to think we'll have anything untoward happen.'

'Mum was in and pretty worried I hear,' Sara said quietly, as she picked up the chart and began looking over it.

'She was okay tonight. Let's face it, it's pretty scary to see a patient for the first time after oral surgery, or any surgery for that matter,' Tom replied, as he watched Sara checking the notes. 'Sometimes we just forget that we're all hard nuts after so many years. Nothing much fazes us.'

After they had checked on George and the other patients, who were settled into the wards, Sara accepted Tom's offer of a lift home. She had left the Lexus at home and walked to the hospital that morning to get some exercise but had no intention of walking home at night. He put the heater on high and Sara snuggled into the seat. She rested her face against the crinkled leather and took deep breaths. Secretly she luxuriated in the scent of his aftershave. It was all through the car. It was like old times.

Tom turned his head and smiled. He knew he had so little time with her he had decided to enjoy every minute. It was hard to be this close when he knew these were the last weeks they would ever spend together. This was it. They would part and he would never see her beautiful face again.

Sara was enjoying Tom's company. There was no tension. No animosity. It was like a truce before they parted ways for ever. The city looked extraordinarily pretty through the fogged glass. Sara knew that her relaxed mood and contentment gave her an appreciation of the normally overlooked sights. The cityscape of high-rise buildings sparkled like brightly coloured fairy-lights against the black sky.

A tram trundled along beside them, the 1920s-style red carriage lit up, and Sara watched the people inside. Businessmen in coloured suits, young women in office attire, a few teenagers and an old lady with a strange feathered hat all sat facing forward as it made its way down Collins Street, rocking a little from side to side.

In the silence of the car Sara wondered for a moment about where they were all going, and if anyone was waiting for them.

It was very cold outside and she was so grateful to be with Tom.

It was like old times. Almost. He walked her to her door and she asked him in for coffee.

'I'll take a raincheck. It's late and I've got a killer of a day tomorrow.' Tom sensed her vulnerability and didn't want to risk a repeat of that night they'd shared not too long ago. He wasn't only protecting Sara from being hurt. He knew he was vulnerable himself.

Sara felt both relief and disappointment when he turned her down. She knew it was best, because she knew she was losing her heart to Tom all over again. It was in both of their best interests that he take control before she lost hers and headed down the right path with the wrong man again.

'Mine's hectic too,' she answered with a short sigh, as she watched him cross the softly lit porch and step onto the loose gravel. 'But being so busy the week is just flying by. I can't believe the weekend's so close.'

He paused and the crunching noise beneath his feet stopped. 'Are you happy for me to drive you to our country christening this weekend?'

'That'd be lovely,' she said. 'I'm so excited to see Dana and Stu, not to mention Bonny and the boys.'

She watched as Tom crossed to his own porch and unlocked the front door. He smiled at her and they stepped inside their respective houses and closed their doors in unison.

On Saturday morning her overnight bag was packed and waiting by the front door ready for the early start, the silver frames tucked safely inside. Unfortunately it wasn't an early start. It was after eleven-thirty before they finally left for the country.

A and E was flat out from the Friday night and Tom had been called in at about six in the morning to help out with an emergency jaw reconstruction.

Tom told Sara about the operation as they drove north along the Hume highway towards Seymour. The sky above them was a clear blue, although soft grey clouds were gathering over the hills in the distance. Sara wound down the window and enjoyed the cool breeze on her face. She had wrapped a light scarf around her hair but the loose wisps were tickling her face.

'What are you smiling about?' Tom asked her. His gaze stayed on her for only a moment before he turned it back to the road.

Sara brushed away the hair, trying to tuck it behind her ears. It was no use. The wind was too strong as Tom increased the speed of the car to climb to the Victorian state limit.

'Nothing, really. I've just got hair all over the place.'

'Then wind up the window.'

She shook her head, sending more of her hair flying about. She couldn't contain her smile. 'No, I'm enjoying it. It feels so good to get away from everything. No pagers, no day lists, no…no schedules to keep!'

Her happiness was contagious and Tom's mouth broke into a broad smile as he put his foot down and took off down the highway.

An hour later they pulled into a roadhouse. It wasn't situated in a town. It was just a petrol station and restaurant on the side of the highway, in the middle of nowhere. There was flat dry scrub for as far as Sara could see. Low bushes and an occasional eucalypt dotted the pale green and brown landscape.

'How about an all-day breakfast?' he asked as he pulled up beside a petrol pump.

'Is it safe to eat here?' She made a wry face as she watched a burly truck driver jump down from his rig. The shiny red cabin door was decorated with a painting of a scantily clad woman. Suddenly the loud noise of another huge semi-trailer pulling in made her jump in her seat. The brakes squealed and then whooshed with the release of air as the huge beast came to a halt behind them.

'It wasn't that I wasn't expecting the Ritz,' Sara shouted over the noise. 'But this looks a little, well, rough around the edges.'

Tom grinned. 'You can guarantee, Sara, if the buses and trucks stop here, then the food will be the best. They can't afford to get gut problems on long interstate hauls. They'll only eat where they know the places are clean and the food is fresh.'

Hesitantly, Sara made her way inside.

Tom was right. The bacon was crisp, the scrambled eggs were deliciously fluffy and the coffee was freshly brewed.

'Dana and Stu's place is only about an hour down the road,' Tom said as he paid the bill and gave his compliments to the chef. He held the door open for Sara. 'I still don't know how he manages to drive in every week for four days and then come home for a long weekend. I like city living and country visiting...once or twice a year.'

Sara nodded in agreement. She was looking forward to spending the next two days on the farm but she couldn't stand the thought of driving that far every week, like Stu did.

'I suppose you can't take the country out of a country boy, can you?' she said as she climbed into the car and pull the door closed. 'Or the city out of us city folk.'

He didn't start the car until the last semi-trailer had pulled out onto the road. There was no point leaving first. The vintage car would only get in the way and force the semis to overtake.

They drove while chatting happily about the practice and the hospital. Soon the town sign appeared. Seymour. It was at the junction of the Hume highway and Goulburn Valley and Sara knew it would be a picturesque part of the country.

Tom turned off the highway into Seymour. The farm was outside of the main town so they headed down Station Street and stopped at the Railway Club Hotel.

'I didn't have time to get any wine for tomorrow,' Tom said, as he climbed out of the car. 'I'll just grab a bottle or two. Would you like anything?'

Sara shook her head. She was still full from their lunch. She looked around as she waited for Tom. It was a typical country town where everyone took their time and knew their neighbours. Sara watched as a group made their way to the river with their fishing gear. It wasn't long before Tom emerged with his purchases and reversed the car and continued down the street.

'How long since you were here?' Sara asked him, as she looked at the heritage buildings dotted along the main road. As they made their way through the town she admired the gorgeous gardens.

'I was only here just over six weeks ago,' Tom answered as he left the town and headed along the Goulburn Valley Highway to the farm. 'I came down with Stu when Bonny was released from hospital.'

'That must have been a dreadful time.' Sara paused for a moment and looked across the huge vineyards that surrounded the township. She was searching for the right words. 'I think seeing Bonny so badly injured and yet being unable to do anything more would have made me feel so helpless. It's so hard when only time can heal someone you care about.'

Tom said nothing but the emotion that poured into his face told Sara everything she needed to know. He still felt the pain of Bonny's injuries, that was obvious. And he still carried those of his brother.

Her heart aching with sadness at what might have been, she turned her gaze away from Tom and back to the scenery. They turned left onto a dirt road and the car bumped along the uneven surface for a half a mile before they found the entrance to the farm.

As they travelled up the last part of the potholed road to the house, Tom filled Sara in about the property. Stu and Dana had bought the house when they'd returned from Queensland. It was more of a hobby farm and a rural escape than a money-making venture.

They had bought a small number of sheep to graze over the few hectares of bush land that had been cleared and a couple of alpacas roamed around to protect the sheep from foxes. In another paddock were some grape vines but these were grown only on a small scale. Selling the grapes to local wine producers made just enough to fund the farm. There was no huge profit in this venture. Dana tended to the general running of the property and had needed to employ only one farmhand, Adrian, who also helped out with any odd jobs that Stu was too busy to deal with.

Sara stepped out in the driveway to hear a kookaburra's call from top of the lofty eucalypts.

'Did you have a good trip?' Stu asked the pair as he

approached them enthusiastically. He had heard them coming up the long driveway and was already outside, waiting for them.

'Tops,' Tom replied, as he closed the car door.

'What about you, Sara? Did you enjoy the bumpy ride in the old Austin Healey?'

'It was great, and it's even better to see you again,' she said, before she wrapped her arms around Stu and hugged his huge bear-like body.

'Dana's in the kitchen,' he told her, patting her back affectionately and walking her to the house. He opened the front door and stepped back, smiling. 'Those godsons of yours have made one hell of a mess in their highchairs. Food all over the place. Looks like a war zone. I was lucky to get out alive the way they were throwing stewed pears and cereal about.'

Dana was as thrilled to see Sara as she was to be there. The pair embraced affectionately.

Sara couldn't believe it had been three years—it felt like yesterday. Dana hadn't changed a bit. Her brown eyes sparkled and her long red hair was still a mass of curls tied back from her pretty face with an antique clasp. She was about Sara's height, which meant she was dwarfed by her husband. Her petite frame was dressed in jeans and a canary yellow overshirt.

The kitchen was big with a true country feel to it. Rows of saucepans and utensils hung down from the ceiling within reach of the workbench and beautiful floral curtains draped the windows. The cupboards and drawers were oak and so was the big kitchen table and chairs. The floor was tiled in aged terracotta and a potbelly stove in the far corner warmed the large room.

Henry was the bigger twin. His brother Phillip was slightly smaller framed, though both had had a shock of red hair. Sara was thrilled to finally see them, and she could hardly wait to see Bonny.

'Where is she?' Sara finally asked, after giving both Henry and Phillip kisses on the tops of their heads. It was the only part of them not covered in food. 'Where's Bonny?'

Dana smiled so widely at the question that Sara was afraid her hostess for the weekend would burst before she told her.

'Dana, what is it? Tell me. Where is she?'

'Horseriding.'

Sara felt the colour drain from her previously flushed face. 'She's what? You can't be serious?'

Dana climbed down from the footstool after wiping the last of the pears and rice cereal from the wall. 'I'm deadly serious. Bonny's out riding her pony, Sheba, with Adrian. And she can talk again. She started speaking only two days ago.'

Sara couldn't believe what she was hearing. Bonny had still been critically ill only a month ago and now she was horseriding and her voice was back.

Dana hurriedly rinsed the checked cloth under running water and hung it over the dish drainer before she sat down at the table with Sara. But her work wasn't done and she reached over and began cleaning Phillip's face. Sara took another facecloth and busied herself with cleaning up Henry.

'It was meant to be a surprise. Bonny didn't want anyone to know she was walking or talking again until the boys' christening party. My mother and father still think she needs a frame to walk and a board to spell the words, and so do Stu's parents. Bonny thought she'd surprise both sets of grandparents by walking into church and singing the hymns.'

'That's wonderful,' Sara told her friend as she finished wiping the last of the sticky mess from Henry's chubby little fingers. He gurgled and gave a toothless grin that immediately brought a smile to Sara.

'Good,' Stu's deep voice called through the wire screen door. 'It's cleaned up. We can get something to eat.'

Dana shook her head as she looked over at Sara. 'Isn't it amazing what impeccable timing men have? It always saves them from the worst scrapes.'

Sara couldn't agree more. After Stu and Tom brought in the bags, putting Sara's in the spare room and leaving Tom's by the door to be taken out later to the guesthouse, the four of them ate lunch with the boys safely placed in a nearby playpen. Dana had prepared open sandwiches, with Sara's help.

'Savour the ones with egg filling,' Stu mumbled cheerily with a mouthful of sandwich. 'Thomasina's laying about one a week, and that's only in a good week!'

They all laughed. They cleaned up and put the boys to sleep before the four of them went out to find Bonny and Adrian. The air smelt good and fresh but the sky was almost covered with ominous-looking clouds. Although a downpour was a while off, the breeze was quite cold and the ground was still heavy from recent rainfall. Sara had worn jeans and a hand-knitted jumper on the car trip so she needed only to grab her scarf, throw her waterproof jacket over the top and slip into some knee-length rubber boots that Dana gave her.

Before they left the farmhouse, Tom took his bag to the guesthouse, not far from the main house, and changed into similar country clothing.

After a few minutes of walking they had reached the small shearing shed near the riding track.

'Uncle Tom, Uncle Tom!' came the excited cry. 'Look at me!'

Sara spun round to see Bonny, all grown up and sitting high in the saddle with her brown riding hat firmly in place, her curly auburn hair tied in long plaits and a yellow raincoat buttoned up against the breeze. Sara felt pure joy as she watched Bonny parade around them on her chestnut coloured pony.

Stu coughed to clear his throat. 'Excuse me, missy. We have another guest.'

Bonny peered down in Sara's direction and pulled Sheba's reins to a halt. 'Aunty Sara?'

'Yes, it's me, Bonny. I'm sorry I've been away so long. Too long.' Sara's throat was choked by emotion. 'It's…it's so good to see you up there. I can hardly believe it.'

Bonny's pretty face was aglow as she began a slow canter around the foursome. 'I'm walking into church tomorrow. Did Mummy tell you?'

Sara nodded. 'She certainly did, Bonny, and I know it's a secret so I won't say a word to anyone.'

'Adrian,' Stu called to the young man who followed closely behind Bonny on a glistening black mare, 'I'd like you to meet a friend of ours.'

Sara watched as he carefully turned the cantering horse and rode over to her.

'Sara, I'd like you to meet Adrian Gorden. Adrian, this is Sara Fielding.'

'Pleased to meet you, Sara,' the boy said politely, but his eyes didn't stray from Bonny for too long. Before Sara had a chance to respond, Sheba moved her head suddenly and Adrian instantly cantered back over to Bonny.

'We'd better head back as there's lots to do before tomorrow,' Dana told them. 'And that includes you, Bonny. You've got some more physio and then a hot bath. You can spend the afternoon inside with the boys.'

'What size boys are we talking about, darling?' Stu asked light-heartedly. 'Have Tom and I been grounded too?'

Dana laughed as she gently reached for Sheba's reins and turned the pony in the direction of the farmhouse. 'No. I guess you two can have the afternoon off. But don't forget you've got lots to do this evening and first thing in the morning.'

Stu saluted his wife and then bent down and kissed her. Sara looked away. The love they shared was almost palpable and it made her feel a little uncomfortable. It used not to, all those years ago, but back then circumstances had been different. That had been when she and Tom had also shared those tender moments and so much more.

'Okay, Tom, looks like we've got a few hours free. How about a trip into town and a pint with some of the locals?'

Sara spent the afternoon chatting with Bonny and helping with preparations for the next day's festivities. Dana's parents would be arriving the day of the christening but spending the night. Stu's family wouldn't stay at all because they only lived in the next town.

Sara's room was already prepared but she helped Dana ready another guest room, putting fresh sheets on the queen-sized bed. This would be for Dana's parents.

Sara offered to go out and prepare Tom's bed in the

guesthouse by herself, leaving Dana free to begin another. It was a small, self-contained unit with its own kitchen, bathroom and bedroom. Dana gave her fresh flowers to put on the table and extra blankets for the bed. It was an odd feeling and she had butterflies in her stomach as she made the bed Tom would be lying in that night. She had to push the feelings away as she tucked in the last blanket corner.

'It's lucky you have such a big place to hold us all,' she said, when she finally came back into the kitchen, where Dana was busily decorating the christening cake. It was a fruit cake in the shape of two booties and iced in the palest powder blue.

The afternoon raced by. Sara was happy to follow Dana's instructions and roll the three dozen chocolate-dipped lamingtons in coconut, blend the cream cheese and salmon for the dip and carefully fold the huge pile of blue and white serviettes. Bonny joined in and helped with the serviettes after her bath. They had decided, with all the party preparations, to leave the physiotherapy until her father returned home.

'How many guests are you expecting, Dana?'

Dana had her head in the fridge looking for the carrots to grate into the coleslaw. 'We've planned on sixty,' she said, as she stood up and crossed back to the sink with the bunch of carrots in her hand. As Sara watched Dana cut off the leafy, green tops and discard them into the bin, she couldn't help but wonder if one day she would be knee deep in preparing a family function for her own children.

The men came home around six o'clock, just in time for dinner. After the delicious meal of roast pork and vegetables, Tom chose to spend some quiet time with Bonny while the others finished their bread-and-butter pudding. He had excused himself before dessert and headed off to play a board game with the excited little girl in the family room.

Sara noticed how much he loved spending time with Bonny and how his self-imposed sentence would rob him of the opportunity to do the same with his own child. But that was his choice, she reminded herself, although it made her sad to think she could do nothing to change it. She couldn't find a way to get through to him and make him see that he was denying himself something so precious.

'It's not like Tom to refuse dessert,' Dana commented as she stacked the emptied bowls. 'He usually eats like a Mallee bull.'

'That's okay. If he doesn't come back for it, I'm happy to eat his tonight. This country air is giving me an appetite,' Sara said, helping Dana to clear the table.

The two women made quick work of cleaning up the dinner dishes, while Stu gave the boys a bottle each and Tom remained out of sight with Bonny. They could all hear the laughter coming from the other room as Tom and Bonny played card game after card game.

'I think we should all play cards tonight. What about bridge or poker?' Dana suggested, as Stu took the two drained bottles away from Henry and Phillip.

'Sounds like a great idea to me,' Stu replied. 'I'll just change my little men here, and then get the children up to bed. Give me ten minutes and then I will clean the lot of you up in a game of poker. Bridge is for sissies.'

Sara smiled. 'Poker it is.'

* * *

They were about forty minutes into poker when Stu felt a headache coming on and thought he might call it a night. Dana said she thought she might head to bed early as well, since it was going to be a big day tomorrow.

'Why don't you two head back into town and get a drink or something? I mean, you are welcome to stay here and watch television, but we are a bit boring in our old age and tend to settle down quite early.'

'We may just do that. What do you think, Sara? Up for a big night on the town?'

Sara was a little tired but thought it might be fun to head into town and see what the locals were up to.

'Sure, why not?' she replied.

'Then that's settled. You will see us later,' Tom announced, as he stood up and slipped his warm jacket on.

Stu reached into his pocket, pulled out his keys and tossed them across the room. 'Take the four-wheel drive. It's safer on the roads out here at night than that antique toy car you drive, not to mention a lot warmer.'

Tom caught the keys and nodded in agreement. Sara went quickly to her room and grabbed a warm coat and scarf.

'I'll drive,' she said with a smile, as she took the keys from Tom's hand and headed outside. The air was freezing as they climbed into the huge four-wheel drive. It took only moments to realise she wouldn't be driving anywhere.

'Change of mind, you can drive after all,' she told Tom, and then climbed out of the car. With a puzzled expression Tom stepped out of his side, walked around to the driver's door and climbed in. They both shut their doors at the same time.

'Of course,' he said, with laughter in his voice. 'You can't drive anything with a manual gearbox!'

Sara nodded sheepishly.

'You know, Sara, it has always amazed me how you can perform complex surgical procedures but can't co-ordinate your feet and hands to use a clutch and gear-stick!' He chuckled to himself and Sara rolled her eyes as they took off down the dirt road, the headlights on high beam.

It didn't take long before they pulled up outside the Royal Hotel.

'Someone told me this was the subject of a Drysdale painting. Is that right?' Sara asked as they quickly made their way to the entrance. It was so cold. There was no breeze but it was like standing inside a cold room and it was chilling them both to the bone.

'I don't know, to be honest, but I'm sure Stu would. You can ask him in the morning,' Tom said, as he held the hotel door open for Sara. He added, 'Not sure about you but I think I would prefer a hot chocolate to a wine tonight.'

Sara nodded in agreement as she blew warm air on her hands and crossed to a table near the fire.

They both enjoyed a warm drink and a light-hearted chat about Stu and Dana and their wonderful property and how amazing Bonny's progress was, considering her injuries.

Sara suddenly realised that she had forgotten to take the spare key Dana had placed in her room, and it was only when Tom looked at his watch that they saw how late it was.

As they pulled back into the driveway ten minutes later, they saw that the main house lights were turned off.

'Looks like they've locked you out,' he said.

'I don't want to wake them, that wouldn't be fair.'

'There's nothing for you to do but spend the night in the guesthouse with me.'

Sara swallowed nervously as Tom unlocked the guesthouse and she followed him inside. It was lovely and warm and Sara guessed the either Dana or Stu had put on the heater for Tom before they went to bed. He turned on the lamps and she could see into the bedroom. She had made the bed earlier in the day, thinking that Tom would be lying between the sheets. That had been hard enough to think about.

She'd never dreamt that she would be lying in the same bed. Or that they would fall asleep together and she would wake in the morning to find his gorgeous face on the pillow next to hers.

Her stomach began tying itself in small knots as Tom removed his coat and slipped his heavy shoes off. When he undid his shirt and told her he was taking a shower, the knots turned to churning and her heart started to pound. She didn't know where to look as he casually dropped his shirt on the chair and slipped his belt from his jeans.

She quickly reached for a book, any book on the coffee table, as his trousers hit the ground and he disappeared in to the small bathroom. She knew there was nowhere in there to place his clothes but removing them in front of her was far too unsettling. Sara put the book back down on the table, completely unaware of what was even on the cover. Her mind was spinning as she went into the bedroom and turned down the bed. She was waiting for Tom to finish his shower when she heard him call out.

'Sara, take my pyjama top to stay warm in bed tonight. I'll wear the bottoms. You'll find it in my overnight bag. And there's a spare toothbrush in there as well.'

Sara felt uncomfortable searching in his belongings but decided if she got the top while he was in the shower then she could change without him seeing her naked. She unzipped the bag and found the top and the toothbrush. Hastily, she slipped off her winter clothes and put on his warm pyjama top. Then she put the pyjama pants on the end of the bed for Tom.

'You can come in and brush your teeth, you know. There's a shower curtain.'

Sara wished she hadn't heard. 'I can wait,' she called back.

'You know I take for ever,' he called over the sound of the running water. 'You could be in bed in five minutes if you can ignore my singing while you floss.'

Sara cringed with the thought. Not at his singing but of him standing naked behind the shower curtain only inches from her. Tentatively, and with an enormous amount of trepidation, Sara opened the door and stepped inside the steam-filled room. Her bare feet crossed the tiles to the sink.

'Almost like old times,' came Tom's voice from behind the curtain.

'Almost,' she muttered, as she squeezed some toothpaste on her brush and bent forward over the basin, beginning to brush her teeth. It was the most disconcerting tooth-brushing experience she could recall.

The curtain suddenly moved back, revealing Tom's head and very naked upper torso. 'Sorry, I couldn't hear you.'

Sara instinctively closed her eyes. Tight. She didn't want to see what she knew was in front of her. The vision of her naked and extremely handsome soon-to-be-ex-husband was not something she could easily, if ever, forget.

She pointed her hand at her toothbrush already in her mouth, hoping he would understand that she couldn't talk. He did and the curtain was pulled back again.

Sara breathed a sigh of relief and finished brushing and flossing in record time. She left the bathroom, calling out goodnight before she closed the door on her way out.

Snug in her oversized nightwear, she climbed into bed. She pulled the blankets up to her chin and tried to push any thoughts of the last time she'd shared a bed with Tom from her mind. She closed her eyes and prayed she would fall asleep quickly. But that didn't happen. Tom stepped from the bathroom with his towel hung low. She didn't want to look at him but she did. In the soft light creeping from under the bathroom door she watched his perfectly sculpted body cross the room to where his overnight bag lay.

'Your pyjama pants are on the end of the bed,' she whispered softly, and again she closed her eyes very quickly and very tightly before he dropped his towel.

She heard Tom thank her before he turned off the heater and the light and slipped into bed.

'Goodnight, Sara.'

She felt his weight on the other side of the bed and the fresh scent of soap as she lay so close to the man she knew she still loved.

She was so confused that it felt so right, so good and so comforting to be sharing Tom's bed. She didn't want to feel that way. She may not have any intention of acting on it, but there was no denying she felt at home and safe in a strange bed because Tom was in it with her.

'Goodnight, Tom.'

* * *

It was about two in the morning when she woke up, feeling a little hungry. There were some cookies that she had spied earlier in the kitchen so she made her way out there quietly. Without making too much noise, she heated some milk on the stove and sat at the small kitchen table, dipping her cookies into the cup. Then she made her way back to the bedroom. The moonlight was shining though the gaps in the curtains, faintly illuminating the room. She noticed he had kicked his covers off. Without thinking too much about it, she instinctively moved to cover him.

Gently she pulled the covers up and over his bare back. He had sacrificed the warmth of his top for her. The room was now cold and she suspected his back would be icy to touch. A bittersweet smile tugged at her mouth as she remembered back to when they had been married and how she would always have to cover him during the night. His shoulders would be so cold to touch but he would be sleeping peacefully, perhaps in the knowledge that she would keep him warm.

He gave a deep throaty moan and startled her. She reeled back on tiptoe, holding her breath. His thick lashes flickered and he scratched his head.

Sara's pulse was racing. What would she say to him if he woke to find her leaning over him?

Thankfully she didn't have to find a hasty excuse. He didn't wake up. He just rolled over, tossing the blankets aside and uncovering himself again. Her breathing became steady but quite loud. For a moment she stood in silence, trying not to make a sound in case she woke him. Sara didn't dare to try covering him again. Instead, she crept back to her side of the bed.

There was a tug in her chest as she quietly slipped

under the covers, knowing she would be spending the rest of her life without him.

In ten short days she would walk away, again. Gone from Tom's life for ever. She would never be there to cover his back.

CHAPTER ELEVEN

DANA AND STU were eating breakfast with Bonny and the boys when Tom and Sara entered the kitchen.

'Morning, guys,' Tom greeted them cheerfully. 'I can tell it's going to be a great day.'

'Morning to you two,' Stu said, swallowing a mouthful of porridge and ignoring the change to sleeping arrangements. 'There's plenty of this on the stove. Unless you'd prefer cold cereal.'

'No. Porridge is lovely,' Sara said, climbing to her feet and getting two bowls from the kitchen dresser. Tom followed behind, taking two spoons from the drawer. They smiled at each other when they realised what they had done. It was like old times.

'Church is at—' Dana cut her words short when she saw the arrival of a huge delivery truck in the driveway. 'What on earth is that?'

Bonny ran to the window to look out as Stu and Dana crossed to open the door.

A uniformed man climbed down from the truck, its side emblazoned with the impressive logo of a large department store in Melbourne.

'I have a delivery for Henry, Phillip and Bonny Anderson,' the driver announced, as he neared the open door. 'I need a signature before I can get the parcel from the truck.'

'There's something for me too?' Bonny screamed excitedly, and hobbled to the door. 'But it's not my birthday or anything.'

Sara shot Tom a puzzled look and then leant over to him. 'You got the boys the bears, didn't you?' she whispered in his ear.

He nodded and smiled as he looked straight ahead. 'And one for Bonny.'

Bonny was bursting with excitement. 'Mummy, can I go out and help?'

Dana ruffled her daughter's mass of auburn curls. 'I don't think the gentleman will need too much help, sweetheart.'

The young man coughed. 'Don't believe it. I could do with some help but definitely adult size for this delivery.'

Stu and Tom followed him outside. It was only a matter of minutes before three chocolate brown, six-foot teddy bears with rotund tummies marched their way down the ramp from the truck.

Sara smiled at the sight of the first two with their checked bow-ties and then the third with a string of pale pink pearls around its enormous neck. The men were all struggling to keep their balance as they carried the trio inside.

Bonny was ecstatic and the boys' little faces lit up and they started gurgling at the sight of their huge furry presents.

'But I'm not being christened,' Bonny said, as she hugged the bear now sitting on the floor. She stood possessively beside it, running her fingers over the monstrous pearls.

'It's a get-well present from Aunty Sara and me.'

'You shouldn't have,' Stu and Dana said in unison.

'I'm glad they did!' Bonny said.

The morning went well. Dana's parents arrived at the same time as Stu's mother and father. The church service was at one o'clock and afterwards everyone came back to the house. Adrian had offered to stay behind to put out the food and see to any last-minute preparations. Dana had organised more than enough food and Stu had seen to the alcohol, so there was no shortage in that department.

'Didn't the boys behave beautifully for the minister?' Sara said, as she offered the plate of sandwiches to Dana's parents. 'Not even a whimper.'

'It was wonderful. I had tears in my eyes the moment I saw Bonny walk into the church and they stayed with me for the entire service.'

'You're too sentimental,' her husband told her. 'I knew our Bonny would pull through. She's a fighter, that's what she is.'

Sara smiled and moved on around the room with the sandwiches and then with the dips and other finger food. Finally, she carried platters of cakes and before too long it was coffee. At around five o'clock the guests started to leave.

Henry and Phillip were fast asleep, unaware of all the fuss for them. Two huge bears sat in the corner of the room, watching over them.

'I almost forgot,' Sara said, carrying a present into the room. 'Tom and I wanted the boys to have something to keep for when they are older.'

Dana unwrapped the parcel with its layers of noisy tissue paper. She gasped. 'They're absolutely beautiful.' Lying in her lap were the two ornate silver picture frames. The family members all gathered around to admire them while Sara started to clean up.

It was about nine o'clock when the mess was under control. They had all picked on the delicious leftovers and were quite full.

'I hate to ruin a nice evening,' Tom said, as he climbed to his feet from the comfortable chair by the pot-belly stove, 'but I'm afraid Sara and I have to head back to Melbourne.'

Tom didn't want to risk anything happening and he was afraid one more night together might cause him to cross the line. He knew Sara had covered him during the night. There had been no need to open his eyes. The warmth in her touch had radiated through his body as she'd pulled the covers gently over him.

It had taken every ounce of his strength not to reach up and pull her into his arms and make love to her. He didn't trust himself. He needed to head back to Melbourne where the boundaries were more defined. Being here with old friends made it even more difficult to remember that he and Sara would soon be divorced.

It would be unfair to both of them, he reasoned, for anything to happen. Sara would be leaving for Texas soon and he would once again be alone with his work.

Sara had made an appointment to see the local general practitioner the next day after work, so she didn't mind heading back early. The tiredness wasn't subsiding so she thought it would be great to have some tests to confirm whether her anaemia had returned.

The next day's patients were straightforward consultations and she left on time to get through the Melbourne peak-hour traffic to the doctor's rooms. She felt great after the two days away but still thought it was prudent to have bloodwork done to rule out anything more serious.

The doctor was a lovely older man and after Sara explained her symptoms he agreed they should do a routine blood test as well as checking her blood pressure and vitals.

'Mrs…I mean, Dr Fielding,' he began, as he undid the blood-pressure sleeve on her arm and folded it back into the pouch on his desk. 'Just run by me your symptoms again.'

'Tired, mostly, and a better appetite than usual. I was up one night recently eating at two in the morning.'

'This may seem obvious but you couldn't by any chance be pregnant could you?'

Pregnant? Sara froze. Of course not. She'd only had sex once in the last eighteen months—the night she'd spent with Tom just over six weeks ago—but they'd been careful.

'Definitely not.'

The doctor eyed her with some degree of doubt. 'So you've not had sex recently?'

'Yes, once more than six weeks ago, in fact, almost seven now, but it was safe, we took precautions. I can't be pregnant.'

'My dear, you're a medical specialist. You know as well as I do that the only one hundred per cent safe sex is no sex.'

Sara was incensed by what he'd said. But it wasn't his tone, it was the fact she knew he was speaking the truth.

Could she actually be pregnant? No, it's not possible, she told herself.

'But there's been no nausea. Nothing. I'm eating well. I think it's more likely my haemoglobin has dropped a little. I've had it happen in the past.'

'Well, I will definitely test for that,' he replied as he completed the pathology request form. 'Is your period late?'

'Maybe a couple of weeks but that's not unusual, I'm not always regular when I'm under stress. I'm moving to live in the US and it's been quite a busy time. As I said, my only complaint is being tired,' Sara said matter-of-factly, not completely sure of who she was trying to convince.

'Not everyone suffers from nausea. Some women go through the entire pregnancy without ever feeling sick, some only feel tired and have an increased appetite, so what if we go ahead and do a simple urine test to rule out pregnancy anyway?'

Sara was unimpressed with the idea. Part of her was suddenly very scared of the result. Part of her already knew the answer. But reluctantly she agreed.

He handed her a specimen jar and walked her to the door. 'The bathroom is the second on the left. Take your time.'

Sara sighed as she walked to the bathroom at the end of the corridor. It was the most nerve-racking walk she had made in her life. Her head was spinning as she thought back to that night. She knew they'd been careful, there had been wrappers on the floor to prove it. She couldn't be pregnant. *Could she?*

Sara already knew the answer. Of course she could. She and Tom made love and now she was taking a pregnancy test.

Sara returned to the consulting room with the sample. The doctor inserted the indicator strip into the jar and they both watched the strip.

It changed colour. It was very clearly blue. There was no doubting it.

Sara's head collapsed into her hands. 'How could this happen?'

The doctor turned and looked in earnest at Sara. 'A baby is not the end of the world, you know, but to make doubly sure I will request the qualitative HCG blood pregnancy test.'

Sara knew that was merely a formality. The strip result was very clear and this type of test was close to ninety-seven per cent accurate.

She was pregnant with Tom's baby.

'We have a pathology unit on hand in the practice to take your blood sample so you can have it done now and the result will come back tomorrow, but as you are already ten days late and with this positive urine analysis I think we can be quite positive that you are indeed pregnant. Although by your reaction I assume this is not something you are going to celebrate,' the doctor said with a sombre tone in his voice. 'There are options. You don't have to proceed with the pregnancy.'

Sara shook her head. 'No,' she answered. 'It's not how I had planned for it to happen but I will be having this baby.' She already loved her unborn child. It had been instantaneous. She loved the child because she loved its father. She knew that, no matter what happened, no matter how Tom reacted to this child, to his child, she would love it for ever and completely.

After the blood test was done, Sara left the consulting rooms in shock. Her heart was beating so fast she could barely breathe. *A baby?* It was a dream come true and terrifying at the same time.

How would she tell Tom? She knew he would be as shocked as her but, unlike her, he wouldn't find any joy in the news at all. Her heart began to beat a little faster and her stomach churned low with anticipation and dread. She knew she needed to tell him. She owed it to him. She paused her racing thoughts and realised it was perhaps not to him but more to the memory of what they had shared. And to finally make a stand. To stop hiding things from each other, no matter the consequences, and no matter what the state of their relationship. It might not be welcome news but he needed to be told the truth.

She also knew she needed time to adjust to the news. A few hours, a day, whatever it took to absorb the enormity of her situation. Her life would never be the same again. And Tom's life would be changed for ever when she told him. Wish as she might for Tom to be overjoyed at her news, there was really no question mark hanging over his reaction. He had made it clear he did not want a child under any circumstances, ever. He was adamant that he would never change his mind.

Sara was so confused. Her thoughts about the pregnancy, her new job in the US and, of course, Tom threatened to overwhelm her on the short trip home. There was so much to consider. Not just her feelings or Tom's, but this child had rights too. The right to know his or her father. Sara pulled into the driveway with her heart still racing.

Her mind was spinning with clashing thoughts as she climbed from the car. She suddenly felt quite faint.

'Sara, wake up,' Tom urged as he stroked her face with a damp hand towel.

Sara's eyes flickered open. She realised she was in her bed.

'What happened?' she asked.

'You tell me. I was inside and heard a thud and went outside to find you collapsed beside the car,' he told her, with his voice filled with concern. 'Are you okay now?' He carefully placed the hand towel on her forehead.

Sara stared at Tom in silence. The reason she'd fainted was not something she intended to share with Tom right now. She needed a little more time. It would only complicate his life and nothing positive would come from it, so she needed to plan how to break the news. She needed to let him know she would be okay no matter what his decision was. Sara knew he would see her pregnancy in a very different light from her.

She reached up for the hand towel, pulled it from her forehead and dropped it onto the bed as she sat up.

'I'm fine,' she replied. 'I did a lot of running around and probably didn't drink enough water. You know me, I have the world's lowest blood pressure on the best of days.'

Tom didn't know what to think but accepted her explanation. 'I'll get you a glass of water.'

'How did I get in here?' she called out. 'I thought you said I passed out by the car.'

Tom reappeared with tall glass of water. 'I carried you inside.' His face was completely serious as he handed her the water to drink. 'You should have a check-up, what with being so tired and now this. You need to get to the bottom of it. I appreciate you've always had low blood pressure, you function on a level that would have most people lying flat out in bed, but please get yourself looked at.'

Sara could see that the concern on his face and in his voice was genuine. But the real reason for her fainting would be too much for Tom to handle so abruptly. They had only just sorted through their complicated past and finally established a relationship free from blame or resentment. An announcement of her pregnancy, she suspected, would probably create both.

She would tell him about the baby. But now definitely wasn't the time.

Sara worked at the practice for the next two days, keeping busy and keeping her distance from Tom. It wasn't hard as his workload had increased steadily with the new student intake.

Sara lay in bed that night thinking about what could have been and the reality of what the pregnancy would mean in her life. She made plans in her mind. She would travel to Paris before she returned to Adelaide to live. When she returned, she would buy a small place in the eastern suburbs of Adelaide to be near to her family. She would work in the hospital or private practice and when she began to show she could say the baby was a result of a holiday romance. A fling with a handsome medico she'd met abroad.

Well, part of it was true at least. Tom was a handsome medico and they had shared a fling. It just hadn't happened in Paris this time.

It was about eight o'clock on Friday night when Sara realised she didn't have any milk. She was still exhausted and didn't want to drive to the grocery store so she thought she would ask Tom if she could borrow some. Warm milk before bed helped her to sleep through the night. She looked out into the drive but there was no sign of his car. Remembering the door between the houses, she found the key in the drawer and unlocked it from her side. She could replace the milk tomorrow.

Sara opened the door and stepped inside Tom's house, reaching for the light switch as she did so.

Immediately, she froze, her gaze falling upon all their old possessions. Everything they'd lived amongst as a married couple. Everything she'd assumed he'd discarded.

The chintz sofa and two matching armchairs. The Persian rug, another honeymoon purchase. The oval card table that was the centrepiece of his living room, an extravagant purchase that had been too lovely to leave in the antique shop in Ballarat on a weekend they'd spent in the country. Sara spun round in shock, her heart racing as she struggled to take in the whole room. Above the fireplace was the beautifully framed triptych print that Stu and Dana had given them for a wedding present, *The Pioneer* by Frederick McCubbin.

Sara roamed dumbfounded through the rest of the house and she found that nothing was missing. When her emotions got the better of her she collapsed into the soft depths of one of the armchairs. She picked up a small hand-painted vase from the tray mobile. Tears blurred her vision as she studied the delicate piece in her hand.

Never in her wildest dreams had she imagined that Tom would be so sentimental.

Being in the house was like stepping back in time.

Sara hadn't taken her belongings when she'd left. She'd thought it would have been too hard to live with pieces of furniture or ornaments that she and Tom had picked out together. Seeing it all now, she knew she had been right. The tears that had pricked at her eyes now flowed freely. It was a strange combination of sadness and regret. And unexpectedly a quiet happiness at being alone with the precious pieces that meant so very much to her and Tom. But, then, she realised, she wasn't alone. She was carrying their child.

Tom was mortified when he unlocked the door and found Sara sitting in the armchair, her head on her hand, as he walked inside.

Embarrassment fuelled his defence. 'What are you doing here?'

Sara quickly wiped her eyes on her sleeve in an attempt to hide her tears. 'I just wanted to borrow some milk.' Her voice was shaky as she felt swept back to the life they had once shared.

'I'm sorry, I didn't mean to upset you.'

After that neither said anything for a few moments.

Tom was trying not to see the sadness in Sara's eyes. He knew she would feel emotional being surrounded by all their past possessions. He had never expected her to see the house.

Sara just sat staring at Tom. There was so much she wanted to tell him, but so much she couldn't.

'Sara...' He broke off for a moment and tried to summon his thoughts. 'I haven't been living with all of this,' he said, gesturing to the furniture.

Her expression was puzzled as he spoke because she didn't understand.

He settled himself into the armchair opposite her and ran his hands nervously over the huge padded armrests. 'I don't live here. This is my spare place. This is where I store everything. For the last three years I've been living the other side, where you are now.'

Sara was even more confused. 'Then why didn't you say so earlier? Why didn't you let me move in here?'

'I felt embarrassed,' he admitted. 'I'd held onto all of this and you'd moved on. I thought you might think it peculiar of me to have kept everything, even after we were over. You didn't want anything when you left and for some strange reason I couldn't part with it.'

Sara sighed as she gently stroked the arms of the chair and then surveyed the room again.

'If you've changed your mind and want anything, please take it. It's yours to have, anything at all,' Tom said, interrupting her thoughts.

Sara bit her lip as she stopped herself from telling him that all she wanted in that room was him. Not furniture, or paintings or ornaments. Tom Fielding, the man, was all she ever wanted.

Tom wasn't sure how Sara felt. He knew she had plans he couldn't change but he hoped that for a while at least they could still keep in touch. He loved every minute he spent with her. That would never change. And until she met someone else, perhaps they could share more time together.

'I was thinking,' he began, as the awkwardness subsided. 'Maybe I could visit you in Texas over Christmas. That is, if you're not flying back to be with your family. But if you're over in a new country and wanting some company, I could check out America for a week or so. I'd have to renew my passport, but if you'd like to spend Christmas with me—'

'Stop it,' she cried out. 'Just stop.'

Sara felt her mind whirling very fast. The thought of Tom visiting and finding her six or seven months pregnant was too much to deal with. The room, Tom, the baby, it was all crashing in around her.

'You can't visit me.'

'Okay, okay,' he replied, in shock at her terse response. 'I just thought...'

Sara couldn't hold it in any longer. She hadn't wanted

to tell him but everything came rushing out, and she found herself close to tears.

'You can't come over because I won't be in Texas at Christmas or ever. I'm not going there any more. I'm going back to Adelaide to be with my family. I'm moving home to live, permanently.'

Tom looked confused and worried. 'Are they all right? Is there something I should know?'

'Yes, Tom, there is something you should know…' Sara paused for a moment. Her heart was pounding, her stomach tightening by the second. Her world was suddenly and completely out of control as the words rushed from her lips. 'I'm pregnant, Tom. I'm having your baby.'

Tom slumped back in stunned silence. He had never thought he would hear those words from Sara. He had never thought he would hear those words from any woman. He had resigned himself to never being a father. His whole world had just changed in an instant. He was shocked to the core. Sara was having a baby. His baby. She was carrying their child. And he knew it would be a beautiful child if it was anything like Sara.

He wanted to rush over and pull her into his arms and kiss her and tell her it was the most wonderful news. But he couldn't. He had to fight his natural instinct, to resist the strongest desire to be with the mother of his child and to protect and love her. He couldn't do either. It wasn't wonderful news. Not to him.

'Aren't you going to say anything?' she asked, not totally surprised by his silence.

He walked over to the window and pulled back the curtains. He was shaking inside. From the moment he'd seen Sara in the restaurant that fateful night, he'd wanted to be with her more than anything he had ever wanted. And now, knowing she was having his baby, he wanted that even more. But he couldn't.

He wouldn't allow himself to share that joy, knowing Heath would never feel the same happiness. Now it wasn't just Sara he had to turn away from, he had to turn away from two people he loved more than life itself. And he hated it that he could never know his own child. They would never meet.

The street was lit by the amber lights and it gave a strange hue to the living room. Sara could see his hand clenching the curtain but still he said nothing.

'Tom, I'm not asking anything from you,' she said honestly, and in not much more than a whisper. 'I know how you feel and I can do this alone. You asked if there was something you should know. Well, there is and this is it. We're going to be parents but I can do it alone. I will move back to Adelaide and get a place near my family. I'll be fine. You don't have to have any part in our child's life, unless you want to.' She rested her hands protectively across her stomach.

He turned to look at her in silence. She was even more beautiful. Perhaps because she was pregnant, perhaps because it was just because he knew she was carrying *his* child.

Tom fought the urge to pull her to him. To wrap his arms around her and tell her that he would protect her for ever. To tell her that he would take care of her, and their baby. But he looked across at the woman who would hold his heart for ever and he knew it would go against everything he believed in. He needed to take responsibility for what he had done to his brother. That would never go away. It was the price he had to pay. And now it was the price they all had to pay. It wasn't fair. Sara and the baby were innocent of any wrongdoing.

His silence was making her feel more uncomfortable by the minute.

Finally he opened up. His soul was being ripped apart but his answer was unwavering. He was steeling himself to push her away. 'You know how I feel about having a child. I explained everything the other night, I opened up about Heath, about the accident, about everything, and you never said a word? Why not then? Why now? Why here in this room?'

Sara was taken aback by the barrage of questions. 'Because I didn't know.'

'And you're absolutely sure you're pregnant?'

'The HCG blood pregnancy test results came back positive three days ago.'

'And you waited this long to tell me?' he asked with confusion in his eyes. 'Three days and you said nothing. There were plenty of opportunities to let me know, Sara. What's different now?'

'Nothing, absolutely nothing. In fact, I wish I hadn't told you at all!'

Sara ran from his house into her bedroom, slamming the adjoining door shut and locking it behind her.

Tom stood in stunned silence. Alone. He was angry. So very angry with himself. For what he was doing to Sara. For the accident with Heath all those years ago. And now for being careless and allowing Sara to fall pregnant. For putting her in the position of having a child that he would never raise.

He knocked on her door.

'We need to talk about this properly. I can't talk to you from the other side of a door.'

He could hear the sound of muffled crying.

'Sara, we can work it out. I will cover the costs of raising the child, I will help in whatever way I can but

I can't live with you and raise this child with you. I just can't be the child's father.'

Sara lay there, listening to the sound of Tom walking away. An overwhelming feeling of sadness engulfed her. One fateful night, when serendipity had brought them together, was now tearing them apart.

The next morning, without saying another word to Sara, Tom left for work early. He needed to keep his distance until Sara left. It was for the best.

He loved Sara with all of his heart. His feelings for her were not in question. But he also knew he wanted more than anything to be the man she needed. To be the father of her child. Not just in name, or financial assistance, but to be the one holding her hand and wiping her brow when their child came into the world. The one to get up in the night and rock their restless baby back to sleep. To take him or her to their first day at school, to sport, to music lessons and everything that Sara had talked about. But he couldn't.

He knew that Sara would be a good mother. And he would ensure the child was provided for financially. The best school, the best medical care if it was needed, the best of everything. But nothing more. He could not be the father she wanted him to be.

He knew he had to let her go. In a few days she would be on a plane and starting a new life with their child. Without him.

CHAPTER TWELVE

SARA DID NOT see or hear from Tom over the next two days. They had managed to avoid each other. She ate her dinner alone. She was leaving on an early evening flight the next day and this was the last night she would be in the house. Sara thought back to the times they had spent together, the tears and passion, the shared memories and professional admiration. The love. She had enjoyed being back in Tom's life, even though it had been only for a little while.

Tom's attitude was noble but cold. Telling her that he would take care of her financially. She didn't want any money from him. She would take care of herself and the baby very well on her own. Financial assistance wasn't what she needed.

But his skewed sense of responsibility wouldn't allow him to be a part of his child's life. The child they had created. The child she would carry for the next eight months. She was pregnant by the man she had loved for so very long and it should have been the happiest time in her life, but instead she was planning her life as a single mother.

But she didn't have time to throw a pity party for herself. She had to move on. And this time for good. No looking back. It would be months before she started to show. She could work until she was six months or even longer. She couldn't tell Marjorie about the pregnancy. She didn't want to explain any of it. She had one more day to work and then she'd be gone. One day of surgery. She had a short morning list and nothing scheduled for the afternoon. The theatre staff were clearly worried when she entered the scrub room.

'Is he operating with you?' the younger of the nurses asked, with wide eyes.

'Do you mean the other Dr Fielding?'

The girl nodded.

Sara shook her head.

The whole operating team gave a sigh of relief and started chatting happily.

'He was like a bull with a sore backside yesterday,' the senior nurse whispered into her ear, as she held the surgical gloves for Sara to slide her hands into. 'We've never seen him like this. No one wants to work with him.'

Sara looked over her shoulder but there was no sign of the man. She knew in her heart that there wouldn't be. Tom didn't want to see her again, let alone work with her.

'Hi,' came a friendly voice. 'Guess what? I get to assist you today. If that's all right with you? I mean, if you'd rather someone—'

Sara didn't have to turn round to know that Nigel was her assisting intern. 'Welcome to the team, Nigel,' she said, as they entered the theatre. For Sara it would be the last time.

The first patient on the list had impacted wisdom teeth. Confident her patient was under the effects of the anaesthetic, Sara began the routine procedure to remove the offending teeth and to suture and pack the sockets. Nigel assisted and took direction well. Sara considered him a competent young surgeon but working with Nigel couldn't come close to being in the surgery with Tom. She knew the comparison was unfair.

Tom had years of experience and Nigel was just beginning his medical career. But it was the way they knew each other's next move. The way Tom's skilled hands would work alongside hers as if their fingers were conversing. As if they shared a single thought. She pulled her gloves and cap free as she took a break following the first patient, just sitting quietly for a few moments. She felt tired but knew after the first trimester the fatigue would be more than likely to pass.

The morning went by without any problems. The cases were all straightforward and Sara was pleased with each and every result. Nigel was chirpy and eager to learn from her. They had finished the last by twelve and after changing into her street clothes and checking her patients in the high-dependency wards she said goodbye to the staff and was gone by one-thirty, heading home to collect her bags and catch her early evening flight in just over four hours' time.

With tears threatening to fall, Sara locked the front door to her home. Her eyes dropped to the crystal slipper in her trembling hand. With one foot nervously placed in front of the other, she took slow steps to his front door. Her chin quivered as she put the slipper and keys in a white envelope and laid it beside his doormat.

With knees bent, she broke down and slumped in tears at his door.

The sound of the taxi's horn brought her to her senses. She wiped her eyes and slipped on her dark sunglasses. The sky was clear blue and, although it was cold, it was bright enough to warrant this disguise.

Sara had planned one stop before she left. She thought she owed Marjorie a goodbye and a thank you.

'I'll miss you,' Marjorie told her. 'Are you sure we can't change your mind about staying?'

Sara had managed to bring her breathing to a steady pace and control her emotions. She wanted to keep it that way.

'No. I'm afraid not. You see, I've made plans to see Paris and then set up a practice back in Adelaide. I miss my family and I think it's the right time to be with them.'

'I suppose Melbourne can't compete with the sights and sounds of Paris,' the woman conceded. 'When do you leave?'

'The plane leaves in just over four hours so I must go—'

'Have a good flight.' Tom's husky voice cut in.

Sara spun round to find him standing very close to her. She wanted to reach out and hold him, to touch his face and feel his arms around her. But he kept a distance between them and she did the same.

'I went home and found you'd left so I thought I'd come in and tidy up.' He took a step back as she turned and she knew better than to close the even bigger space he had created.

With tears moistening her cheeks, she looked across at the man she loved. Marjorie left them alone and busied herself in her office, closing the door behind her to give them privacy to say goodbye.

'I hope I've left everything in order.'

'I'm sure you have.' He said nothing about the tears, which he couldn't have missed.

'Take care, Tom.'

'You too, Sara, and if you need anything just call.' Tom wanted to hold her but he knew that it would break him. He would make a promise he couldn't keep, just so she would stay a little while longer. That would be selfish. 'I'll stay in touch and when the time comes I will provide you with whatever you need or want. I promise you.'

'I'll be fine,' she reassured him. But she wouldn't turn to face him. She didn't want to look into his deep grey eyes. It was over. Finally over. He clearly had no problem with her leaving.

She had no idea what she would be doing in a month. Except trying to start a life somewhere without him.

'Sara, you will never want for anything.'

Except for a husband and a father, she thought as she walked away.

Squaring her shoulders the way she had when she'd first arrived, Sara made her way to the door. She knew Tom was watching her. She willed him to chase after her and ask her to stay.

He didn't.

He let her go.

Tom stood by the window of his office, thinking about nothing but Sara. He had tried to distract himself with paperwork. It hadn't worked. So he'd walked to the window where he had been standing staring at the same static view for the best part of an hour.

It was worse, much worse, he decided, losing Sara a second time. And now he wasn't just losing Sara. He was losing much more.

Sara would be raising a child who was a part of

him. It tore at his heart that he wouldn't be there with them both.

Tom paced in front of the office window. He didn't want to think about Sara raising the child alone. He wanted to be with her. To hold her and their child every day for the rest of his life. He felt an aching regret for all he had said, and all he hadn't. How he had just let her leave. He couldn't live without her. But his brother weighed heavily on his mind too. He felt trapped.

Standing there alone in his office, Tom suddenly realised he couldn't do it. His heart was breaking. She deserved so much more. She deserved to be loved.

He had to stop her.

He couldn't and wouldn't let her go. Not this time.

He had to tell his brother. He had to face those demons from his past and apologise for the hurt he had inflicted. He had to admit his responsibility but tell Heath that now, after all these years, he had another responsibility that he would not walk away from. A far greater responsibility.

Tom finally realised that nothing he did would reverse the result of their actions as teenagers. Sara was right. He would let Heath know he was about to become an uncle and accept whatever Heath wanted to say, good or bad. He couldn't sacrifice Sara and the baby for the sake of a few brief moments that had gone terribly wrong so many years ago. Sara had told him she wouldn't make any more sacrifices, and he wouldn't let her.

He had too much to lose by letting Sara leave again. He wouldn't do it. Not today or ever. He would tell Heath how very sorry he was about what had happened but that he refused to lose the love of his life because of his own unwillingness to put the past behind him.

Tom reached for the phone. He had to do it for his child, and for his wife. He was hurting the woman he loved. And he would hurt the child she was carrying if he didn't stop it now.

With trepidation he dialled the number in San Francisco. He knew it was late at night but he couldn't wait for a better time. There would never be a better time than now.

'Hello,' came Heath's voice down the line.

'Hi, brother, it's Tom.'

'Since I don't have any other brothers I'd guessed that one, old man,' Heath responded in a light-hearted tone. 'What can I do for you? Must be urgent to be calling at this hour.'

Tom didn't know where to start. His brother's joviality unnerved him further. He knew he was going to be delivering a blow and he wasn't sure how to begin. It was the hardest call he had ever made. The culmination of years of guilt and blame. Tom felt his chest tighten. He was about to tell a man who had been robbed of the chance of ever being a father that he was going to have a child with a woman he had always loved and would love for ever. A woman he could not let go. Tom's throat went dry before he spoke.

'Sara's pregnant.'

There was silence on the phone. Tom felt a cold sweat rush over him.

'God, that's got to hurt. I know you still love her, so who's the lucky guy?' Heath said. 'Do you want me to help you take him out?'

'No, you don't need to take anyone out. It's me. I'm the father.'

There was silence again. Tom felt his stomach knot. He wasn't sure what reaction would follow.

'Awesome news. So you two are back together, then, I assume. I'm happy for you both. Congratulations!' Heath answered with elation colouring his sleepy voice. 'Sorry, Tom, I had to leave the bedroom. I'm not alone. Tory's here and I didn't want to wake her.'

Tom was surprised. Not that Heath had a woman there but that he'd never mentioned in previous calls that he was seeing anyone.

'It was one of those rare nights Tory's parents take the children so we get an uninterrupted night together and a lie-in tomorrow morning. That's a hint…don't call again unless it's an emergency.'

'Tory?'

'I'm sure I've mentioned her. We've been seeing each other for almost five months now.' Heath dropped his voice to not much more than a whisper. 'I'm going to ask her to marry me.'

Tom was stunned into silence. Happy for his brother but stunned into a mute.

'I'm the luckiest guy in the world!'

'I'm happy for you,' Tom began. 'But I never thought of you as lucky. Particularly after the accident…that I caused.'

'Tom, don't tell me you're not still harping on about that? For God's sake, man, that wasn't your fault. It was me, a bike and an asphalt BMX run.'

'I know what you're saying but I caused it.'

Heath's voice became a little louder. 'You can stop taking credit right here and now. I had, and still have, the power to exercise free will. I used it that day and I continue to use it every day. I chose a risky trick and it went wrong, but…' he paused '…that was my fault, with maybe some assistance from the universe. Just all-round bad timing.'

Tom felt the tightening in his chest loosen a little. 'But when the IVF didn't work...'

'And now you think you're to blame for my marriage breakdown?'

Tom nodded into the phone.

'You have been thinking way too much, little brother. I can't believe you've been stewing over all this. The marriage broke down because we were unhappy, unsuited and unhappy. We were trying to have a baby as a solution to a marriage with a million flaws. We stupidly thought a baby would be the glue to hold us together. That would have been the biggest mistake. I am so grateful it never happened. It would have been the child who paid the price in the end, living with two unhappy parents.'

Tom had had no idea. This was not what he'd expected to hear.

'And then I met Tory. The most wonderful woman in the world. Her husband was a marine. He was killed on a tour of duty in Iraq about three years ago. She's the best mother and just the most caring soul I could ever meet. And she doesn't want any more children. She had four. And it's a bonus that I don't have to have the vasectomy that she was going to ask me to undergo, until I broke the news about my fertility issues.'

Tom was elated beyond belief. Knowing his brother was in a great place made his decision so much simpler. They were both in love with wonderful women.

'As much as I would love to chat, it's after midnight here so I am going to say goodnight now and call you tomorrow. We rarely get a night to ourselves so I'm not about to spend it on you,' he laughed. 'Please say big congrats to Sara and can't wait for you guys to meet Tory and the girls. I did tell you I'm going to be the stepfather of four daughters, didn't I? I'm going to need a shotgun to keep the boys away if they are as gorgeous as their mum.'

With that he hung up, leaving Tom looking at the phone and wondering why he had wasted all this time.

He wasn't about to waste one minute more.

'I've been such a fool. An idiot of grand proportions,' he said to Marjorie as he rushed into the office and grabbed his car keys. 'You don't happen to know Sara's flight details, do you?'

'You're in luck. I overheard her call to the travel agent the other day and, being the busybody I am, I jotted it down,' she answered with a huge smile, as she pulled a scrap of paper from her pocket. 'It's flight three-five-two, gate seven, and hurry.'

He leant over, grabbed the paper and kissed her forehead on the way. 'Thank God you're a busybody.'

'Your ticket or booking confirmation, please, and your passport, Dr Fielding.'

Sara took a deep breath and reached for both from her carry-on luggage. Her travel agent had secured her a first-class ticket to Paris. *The city of love?* Sara knew that wouldn't be the case this time but it would fit her story perfectly. A fling that had resulted in a baby. Perhaps she would say her lover was a diplomat and he'd been forced to return to his homeland; or a politician; or…or… Sara couldn't think properly.

She would make up a story that wouldn't cause a scandal or embarrass her child. Also one that wouldn't have her child hurting for a father who didn't want to be in their lives. She never wanted her child to know that Tom had let her go. He'd let the two of them leave his life. No child deserved to think they weren't wanted and loved.

Sara rubbed her temples as she waited for her boarding pass to be issued. There was so much to plan and consider.

Tom raced through the traffic, rechecking his watch every few minutes, hoping that he would make it before Sara boarded the plane.

'Last call for passengers on Qantas flight three-five-two for Paris. Now boarding at gate seven.' The voice echoed across the international airport lounge. It was Sara's flight. This was it. For the last two hours she had sat alone in the terminal, thinking about the last six weeks. It was supposed to be a quick trip to the embassy, then a month taking care of Stu's practice. How was she supposed to know that she was already pregnant with Tom's baby when she'd arrived?

Sadness wasn't consuming her any more. The ache in her heart was lessening. She had a new life to cherish and she was in love with the baby she was carrying. She felt blessed to be having a child by the man she loved, even if he wasn't going to be a part of their lives.

Although it wasn't sadness she felt for herself—she felt sorry for Tom. He would never have any part in the life of the child she was carrying. None. He would miss out on so much joy. And love.

But she couldn't spend her life thinking about Tom Fielding. Not even another day. She had to accept what had happened and pretend that she didn't love Tom with all her heart. Until it was true. Until she had no feelings for him. She had to move on and raise their child.

There was no turning back. She knew it would be a

very long time before she returned to Melbourne. She would visit Stu and Dana one day in the future but it would take time. Time to heal the wounds. Time to build a new life…with her child.

Her head down, she made her way slowly to the departure gate. Her boarding pass was in her hand, although her heart was still nowhere to be found.

'Sara,' a familiar voice called out across the departure lounge. 'Stop, don't get on the plane!'

Sara swung her head round but there was only a sea of unfamiliar faces. No one she recognised…until he appeared. Jostling his tall frame though the throng of people. It was Tom. Desperation in his eyes, he made his way over and pulled her into his strong arms.

'I'm so sorry,' he whispered. 'I love you and I was stupid for so long. But not stupid enough to let you go again.'

Sara was dazed. She had no more tears left.

'I want you and our child more than you can ever know. I've been a fool.'

He kissed her mouth and pulled her closer still.

'There's so much I need to tell you, but the most important thing is to ask you for forgiveness for the pain I have put you through. I have been so caught up in doing what I thought was right I've made even bigger mistakes. In trying to right an injustice to Heath, I committed an even greater injustice to you. I was a fool of the biggest kind.'

Suddenly Sara pulled herself free from his arms and stepped back away from him. She closed her eyes for a moment to try and gain some composure. 'Am I dreaming this? What are you doing, Tom? You chase me down and a minute before I fly away you tell me that you want me and our baby. Why? What's changed?'

'Me,' he said, with the conviction of man who knew where he wanted and needed to be. 'I've changed, Sara. I know I was stupid, putting principles before us. Before our happiness and the happiness of our child. I said that I needed to take responsibility for something that happened decades ago but I was letting you leave to bring up our child alone. That's not taking responsibility.

'What I did as a kid was reckless but to let you walk away, to never hold my child and tell him or her that they were wanted and loved would be far more irresponsible. I want you, Sara, I've always wanted you. And I want this baby, our baby, with all my heart.'

She looked at Tom and wanted so much to believe him but she didn't trust her heart. It had led her down the wrong path before.

'I've been living with a misplaced sense of guilt, and hurting you in the process. I was turning my back on the woman I love. I was driving you away. Please forgive me.'

She sat motionless for a minute, thinking about everything he had said, before she finally reached her hand across to his and nodded.

Sara looked into the eyes of the man she loved and knew he was telling her the truth. He kissed her again, and again and again, and held her in his arms for the longest time. He was happier than he had ever thought possible.

Finally he picked up her carry-on luggage and holding her hand tightly in his own, they walked away from the departure gate.

Sara stopped suddenly again. 'How did you get here, into the international terminal, without a ticket?'

Tom held up a boarding pass. 'I organised a ticket to Paris on my way here. I thought it would give me twenty-something hours to convince you to come home with me.'

Sara kissed him with tears streaming down her face.

Tom slipped her crystal keyring into her palm and closed her trembling fingers around them.

'Just promise me, Cinders, that you'll never leave me again.'

'Cinders?' she said, with eyes still bright from her tears. 'You knew about the keyring?'

'I've always known, Sara. It was another reason why I loved you. But I always felt I let my side of your crazy fairy-tale down.'

'You could never let me down,' she cried. 'Unless you let me go.' She met his kisses and melted into his arms.

'Then I promise you, Sara Fielding, you will never be let down again.'

* * * * *

ROMANCE

Ravelli's Defiant Bride	Lynne Graham
When Da Silva Breaks the Rules	Abby Green
The Heartbreaker Prince	Kim Lawrence
The Man She Can't Forget	Maggie Cox
A Question of Honour	Kate Walker
What the Greek Can't Resist	Maya Blake
An Heir to Bind Them	Dani Collins
Playboy's Lesson	Melanie Milburne
Don't Tell the Wedding Planner	Aimee Carson
The Best Man for the Job	Lucy King
Falling for Her Rival	Jackie Braun
More than a Fling?	Joss Wood
Becoming the Prince's Wife	Rebecca Winters
Nine Months to Change His Life	Marion Lennox
Taming Her Italian Boss	Fiona Harper
Summer with the Millionaire	Jessica Gilmore
Back in Her Husband's Arms	Susanne Hampton
Wedding at Sunday Creek	Leah Martyn

MEDICAL

200 Harley Street: The Soldier Prince	Kate Hardy
200 Harley Street: The Enigmatic Surgeon	Annie Claydon
A Father for Her Baby	Sue MacKay
The Midwife's Son	Sue MacKay

0514GEN STD HB

Mills & Boon® Large Print
June 2014

ROMANCE

A Bargain with the Enemy	Carole Mortimer
A Secret Until Now	Kim Lawrence
Shamed in the Sands	Sharon Kendrick
Seduction Never Lies	Sara Craven
When Falcone's World Stops Turning	Abby Green
Securing the Greek's Legacy	Julia James
An Exquisite Challenge	Jennifer Hayward
Trouble on Her Doorstep	Nina Harrington
Heiress on the Run	Sophie Pembroke
The Summer They Never Forgot	Kandy Shepherd
Daring to Trust the Boss	Susan Meier

HISTORICAL

Portrait of a Scandal	Annie Burrows
Drawn to Lord Ravenscar	Anne Herries
Lady Beneath the Veil	Sarah Mallory
To Tempt a Viking	Michelle Willingham
Mistress Masquerade	Juliet Landon

MEDICAL

From Venice with Love	Alison Roberts
Christmas with Her Ex	Fiona McArthur
After the Christmas Party...	Janice Lynn
Her Mistletoe Wish	Lucy Clark
Date with a Surgeon Prince	Meredith Webber
Once Upon a Christmas Night...	Annie Claydon

0514 GEN STD LP

ROMANCE

Christakis's Rebellious Wife	Lynne Graham
At No Man's Command	Melanie Milburne
Carrying the Sheikh's Heir	Lynn Raye Harris
Bound by the Italian's Contract	Janette Kenny
Dante's Unexpected Legacy	Catherine George
A Deal with Demakis	Tara Pammi
The Ultimate Playboy	Maya Blake
Socialite's Gamble	Michelle Conder
Her Hottest Summer Yet	Ally Blake
Who's Afraid of the Big Bad Boss?	Nina Harrington
If Only...	Tanya Wright
Only the Brave Try Ballet	Stefanie London
Her Irresistible Protector	Michelle Douglas
The Maverick Millionaire	Alison Roberts
The Return of the Rebel	Jennifer Faye
The Tycoon and the Wedding Planner	Kandy Shepherd
The Accidental Daddy	Meredith Webber
Pregnant with the Soldier's Son	Amy Ruttan

MEDICAL

200 Harley Street: The Shameless Maverick	Louisa George
200 Harley Street: The Tortured Hero	Amy Andrews
A Home for the Hot-Shot Doc	Dianne Drake
A Doctor's Confession	Dianne Drake

0614GEN STD HB